The Forgotten Island

THE FORGOTTEN ONES

BOOK 1.5

FREYA VICTORIA

First edition April 2024

ISBN 979-8-9893882-4-0 (paperback)

ISBN 979-8-9893882-3-3 (ebook)

ISBN 979-8-9893882-5-7 (audiobook)

www.freyavictoria.com

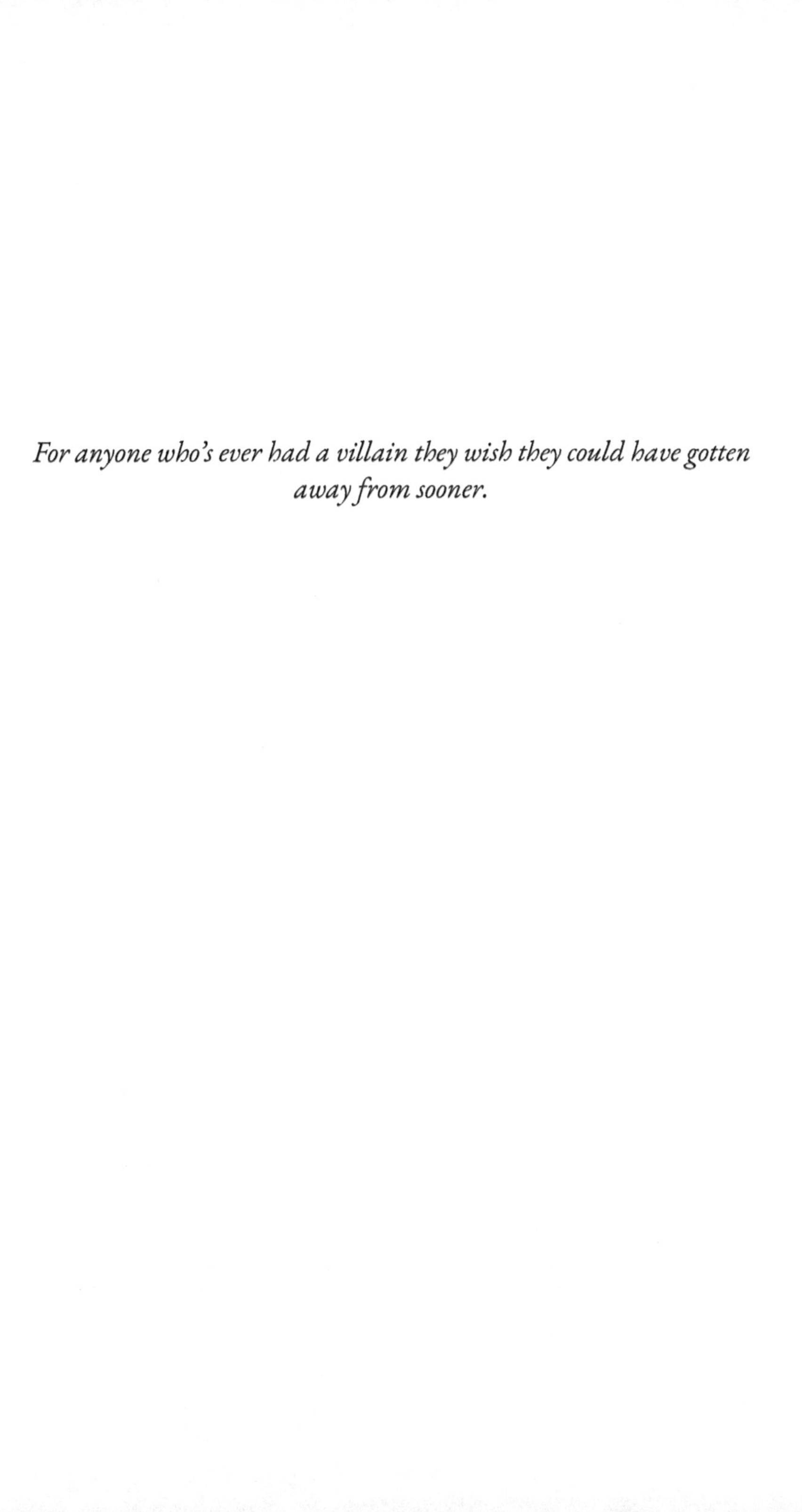

For anyone who's ever had a villain they wish they could have gotten away from sooner.

"Dreams do come true, if only we wish hard enough. You can have anything in life if you will sacrifice everything else for it."
—— **J.M. Barrie, Peter Pan**

Author's Note

POTENTIAL TRIGGERS IN THIS BOOK

The Forgotten Island is a Peter Pan retelling. I want you going into this knowing what you're getting. Ultimately, I want you to protect your mental health and there are absolutely no hard feelings if you need to DNF The Forgotten Island. If you would like a more thorough explanation of any of these, you can find it on www.freyavictoria.com on the book page for The Forgotten Island or you can go to the Trigger Details at the end of the book so you can decide if it's safe for you or not.

This book includes situations with abusive relationship, alcohol, assault, bullying, cheating, child abuse, death, emotional abuse, murder, rape

PART ONE

The Beginning

CHAPTER 1

Fire Up the Night

HOOK

Fucking. Peter.

This morning he sent Wendy off to the castle on the other side of the water, telling her some shit about needing to have a man on the inside. According to him, "You're the only one they won't recognize." He may not be wrong, but that doesn't mean she should have been sent alone.

Okay, maybe not completely alone. But sending her along with her dumbass brothers to infiltrate, or attempt to infiltrate, the castle was beyond stupid. What if they recognize those two idiots?

It's been hours, and she hasn't been back. He probably didn't even take into consideration that if she gets this job, she has to move into the fucking mountain. It takes several hours to ride around the water to get there.

Let's not forget the fact that Peter has done his best to convince everyone the other side is full of shape-shifting demons that eat children. Thank fuck Wendy isn't that easily convinced. But what if she starts to believe the lies?

I pace up and down the passage when I spot Lucia watching me.

"If you're in need of something to keep you busy, I have something in mind that would keep both of us... occupied." I smirk and duck into the nearest room, leaving the door open behind me, giving her the opportunity to just continue past.

I move further into the room, away from the light coming from the passage to the shelves on the other end. One arm stretches above me, my hand resting on a shelf as I wait.

Moments later, I hear the door close, followed by the sound of her quiet breaths.

Turning around, I watch as she makes her way to me in what I imagine she must think is some kind of seductive walk. In reality? I couldn't give less than a fuck what woman is walking in here toward me, because it's not *her*.

I forcefully push Lucia to her knees in front of me and she instantly gets to work pulling out my cock and making some insipid sound before taking me into her mouth. My hand grips the shelf behind me and I close my eyes, imagining the lips I truly want to be wrapped around me right now.

When I glance down and see she's trying to get some kind of friction on her pussy, I wind my fingers into her hair, urging her up.

My lip quirks up at the sound of my cock popping out of her mouth.

I tug her skirts up as quickly as I can before spinning us around and lifting her. She wraps her legs around my waist just the way I like, and I use my body weight to press her into the bookshelf, propping her on its ledge. In one plunge, I'm seated inside her. A yelp escapes her and I swiftly bring my lips to hers to stifle any sounds that will ruin my mood.

My eyes shut, I continue to plunge in and out, feeling my release grow closer and closer, but *just* out of reach. I pull back from her and wrap my hand around her throat, applying just enough pressure to either side, just the way I know Lucia likes it. If I can't get there, I'll be damned if I leave her unsatisfied, too.

Behind her head, I notice a mirror sitting on the shelf. Thank fuck Lucia also wishes she were with someone else, and currently has her eyes closed, or she'd see that we have an audience.

I hold our intruders' gaze in the reflection as I continue to slide in and out of the wet heat engulfing me. My eyes dip to coral lips dropped open in shock, perhaps horror. Who the fuck knows? What I do know is she hasn't moved an inch since her eyes met mine in the mirror.

My orgasm builds and I move my hook to work slow, careful circles on Lucia's clit with the arch. When her moans grow louder, fingers dig into my arms, my shoulders, my back, pulling me closer, urging me on in my movements.

One, two, three more passes across her sensitive flesh and finally her orgasm crests. I pull out as my own slams into me and Wendy's eyes grow wide in the mirror.

It's only then Wendy slips back out the door, closing it silently behind her.

I slowly lower Lucia back to the floor. As I tuck myself back into my pants, she smooths her skirts back around her. She turns and looks in the mirror to fix her hair before moving past me toward the door.

"Until next time," she says, closing it behind her.

I glance briefly in the mirror, but because my hair is always mussed, you can't even tell I recently exerted myself. I've never come so hard, and that was just with her in the room. Unfortunately, I'll never know what it's like to be inside her because she's not free. Wendy Darling made her choice to spend her time with that fucking moron, Peter.

This world is not ready for what would happen if Wendy did ever come to me. We would fire up the night and burn this world down for revenge against him and all he's done to us over the years.

It takes only a few steps before I'm opening the door, and just on the other side, there she is. Her brown hair falls around her, and she bites her lower lip.

"Like what you saw?"

She gasps before clenching her jaw and responding, "Peter is waiting for us in the dining room." She turns around, making her way down the hall. I follow behind at a respectable distance.

My fingers twitch at my side, and I tuck them into my pocket to avoid doing something stupid, like grasping her elbow and showing her just what it feels like to be cherished. He treats her like a damn possession. If there's one thing I've known since before we got banished to this damn world, it's that he is the one person you do your best not to anger. You never know just how he'll react.

Peter. Fucking. Pan. Has been the bane of my existence as long as I've known him.

We round the corner to the great hall and there the prick stands, one hand firmly grasping whatever his drink of the moment is, the other gesticulating wildly as he tells the story full of lies to everyone in our castle.

Fucking Peter with his stupid blond hair and deceptively childlike face. There's a mischievous gleam in his gray eyes before he continues to manipulate them with his poisonous, honey-coated words.

"So there I was in the forest when I saw it." He leans forward and the women and children lean in further than the men. "The wolf transformed into a man and made his way into the village."

Who fucking knows if even that part of the story is true, but there have been multiple spottings of the man who can transform into a wolf.

"I hid in the trees and continued to watch the village, waiting to see what he would do next. In the minutes that followed, there was an uproar in the silence and he came striding out of the village, a child under each arm."

Around the room, gasps can be heard and the women cover their children's ears as he continues to spin the lies.

"Just a few feet in front of me, he snapped their necks and then transformed into the wolf to consume their flesh."

The men who know the truth of the matter show their usual theatrical amount of outrage at the falsehood.

"I will always do what needs to be done to protect all of you from the shape-shifters and their evil ways."

The eyes of the rest of the crowd show gratitude as they nod their heads in assent.

"That will be all today. If you'll excuse me, I need to have a private word with Hook and Wendy," he says before motioning us to follow him into another room.

He stops and turns to us. One hand still holds his glass, the other hand is tucked in his pocket.

"Hello, Wendy dear, I sincerely hope, for your brother's sake, you've got some good news for us." When he pulls his hand from his pocket and extends it to her, she hesitates for the briefest of moments before moving to his side.

Wendy leans in and he turns to face her, but it's my eyes he focuses on when he pulls her against him and gives her a rougher than necessary kiss.

He keeps his arm around her, pulling her into his side before asking, "Did you get the job?"

Her eyes connect with mine before a blinding smile appears on her beautiful face. "I got it."

CHAPTER 2

Up

WENDY

Nicole chatters away while I sit on our bed. My eyes follow her around the room as she helps me pack my things for my stay in the other side's castle.

My mind drifts back to the library, Lucia's moans while Hook had her up against the bookcase. I've never felt so overcome during sex to be unable to keep sounds like that from escaping me. It's more like I just lie there and pray Peter finishes as quick as possible so I can get back to whatever task he interrupted with his need for release.

An added bonus to spending some time in the enemy castle, I don't have to worry about Peter ambushing me every hour of the day. It seems things are finally looking up for me.

What he hopes to accomplish in this little adventure, I'll probably never know. But according to him, in the last letter Tink sent us, things are about to change and we have to be extra vigilant.

"...so then she said that Hook is the best lay in the castle."

My head jerks up and I start to pay attention to what she's saying. "Wait, what?"

"I know, ridiculous, right? Can you imagine having to

maneuver around that hook?" She shudders before returning to fold one of my dresses.

I stand and help her pack the rest of my things for my departure tomorrow. It takes both of us in a synchronized attempt of bouncing on the lid of the trunk to get it to stay closed.

Worn out from our efforts, we lie back on our bed, trying to catch our breath before we both burst out into giggles.

"I'm going to miss you," Nicole says.

"Me too, so much." We stand and I pull her into a hug. "Take care of our people for me, okay?" I whisper before pulling away.

"Of course. I'll do anything for you after you let me share your room so I didn't have to bunk with Lucia." She shudders and I grasp her hand, pulling her behind me as we make our way to the dining room for dinner.

Settled in the wagon between my brothers, I am grateful I could get out this morning before Peter rolled out of bed. We jostle along the dirt trail around the water, each of us lost in our own thoughts.

"Hi, my name is Jimmy. What's yours?"

I look up from my dolly to see who's talking to me. He looks to be about my age and stares down at me, holding his hand out stiffly for me to shake. Carefully, I get to my feet, holding my doll close to my chest with one hand and extend my other to him.

"I'm Wendy."

He squints his eyes as he looks at me. "You don't look gross."

"What? Who told you I was gross?" I drop my dolly to the ground and hold my fists on my hips.

"Everyone knows girls are gross." He rolls his eyes before continuing. "But I think we're going to be the best of friends."

John runs by us, trailing one of Michael's toys behind him, and Michael stumbles, trying to keep up.

"Who's that?" Jimmy asks.

"Just my stupid brothers." I huff out a breath and watch as he reaches down and grabs my dolly off the ground.

He brushes the dirt off of her before holding her out to me.

"Thank you," I say.

"James! Where the fuck have you run off to?"

We both turn toward the man yelling from a house a few doors down from mine.

"I've got to go," he says.

"It was nice meeting you." I feel the heat move up my cheeks as I watch him.

"If you'd like, you can walk with me to school tomorrow. I know the way. I've been walking all by myself since I was five." He walks backward toward his house, awaiting my response.

"I'll ask my mummy if that would be okay. See you tomorrow then?"

"James, if you're not in this house in the next ten seconds, you know what will happen!" the angry man from inside the house yells.

"Bye, Wendy," Jimmy says and immediately turns and runs up the steps of his porch and into his house.

The mountain gets bigger and bigger as we get closer to the entrance while the sun shines overhead.

I turn to John and ask, "How have you both kept your identities secret all this time?"

"Dear sister, no one gives a fuck about the hired muscle," he replies.

"We just make sure not to stir up too much trouble when we're on that side of the line," Michael adds.

"And always remember, the wolf reports back to the king, so don't forget yourself when you're in his presence," John interjects.

He tugs on the reins to slow the team at the same entrance I passed through yesterday.

A man approaches and greets, "Good afternoon, miss. You must be the new kitchen maid?"

"I am." I nod to him and he extends his hand to help me down from the wagon.

"My name is Theodore, I am the steward of the castle. If there's anything you need while you're here, never hesitate to let me know."

I pull my hand out of his, my nerves causing my palms to sweat. As nonchalantly as I can, I smooth my skirts around me, wiping away most of the dampness.

"Joe, Ralph," he greets my brothers with a nod. Well, that answers that question. I wonder if John and Michael thought of the secret identities or if that was Peter's idea?

They return the greeting before lifting my trunk down from the wagon and carrying it between them as we all follow Theodore into the mountain.

A couple of weeks later I've familiarized myself with most of the castle under the mountain. I missed the Thanksgiving celebrations last week in Peter's castle. I have yet to meet the other king, but as I stand in the kitchen waiting for the tray of food for him, I wonder what he'll look like.

When the last item is on the tray, I carefully lift it to my shoulder and make my way to where I'm directed, carefully opening the door and silently setting the tray on one of the tables.

I gasp when I see a woman standing in front of the bookcases. All over my body, my hair stands on end, and I know this is the woman they have sent me here to find.

My brothers return for me soon after the library spotting and again we make our way around the water and back to our castle.

The distance is far enough that it would be hard to tell from the castle in the mountain where exactly it is we head off to. It could be Peter's castle, or we could be heading off somewhere into the vast forest that surrounds us.

When we get to the entrance, I quickly jump out of the carriage and make my way to the doors.

Unlike my arrival at Mason's castle, which I have since learned is the other king's name, no one is here to greet me when I enter.

I hurry down the halls looking for someone, anyone, to tell the information I've been able to glean over the past couple of days concerning the world's newest occupant, Callie.

I hear raised voices and I make my way toward them, pressing my ear to the door just to be sure before grasping the handle and opening it.

Peter and Hook stand on either side of the room. Their heads turn toward me when I enter. Both men take deep breaths as they compose themselves.

"Good evening, gentleman. Miss me?"

Hook smirks and holds my gaze while Peter approaches me from the other side, spinning me and dipping me before his lips descend on mine. To avoid a scene, I part my lips, allowing his entrance as he plunges his tongue into my mouth.

PART TWO

Why Are We Getting Ready for War?

CHAPTER 3

Laid

PETER

When I pull my lips away from hers, I ask, "So tell us, Wendy, what news do you bring from the other castle?"

She takes time to stand up straight, and I don't miss the step away from me she takes before responding, "I found her."

Three little words and my mind immediately starts spinning, thinking about all the moving parts I need to put into motion before following the rest of the instructions in the letter. "We need to gather our men," I address to Hook.

He nods before he glances once more at Wendy.

"That will be all," I snap, and he immediately makes his way out.

Wendy bites her lip, her gaze directed at the door. I grip her hand in mine before weaving my fingers in her hair and tugging her head back, forcing her to look at me. "Wendy, dear, you've been gone an awful long time. I've missed you."

With my other arm, I pull her against me, the sweet pressure against my aching cock driving me crazy. "Why don't we go take care of that? It's about time I get laid." She quickly shutters the flash of indignation before she slowly starts to tug her skirts up. "No, darling, not here."

She follows me through the halls as I grip her hand tightly in mine, forcing her to run to keep up.

When we make it to my bedchambers, she resists briefly before entering the room. I shove her down on the bed and she gets her skirts out of the way. I pull out my cock and stroke myself before tugging her to the edge of the bed and thrusting deep.

I move in and out, enjoying the feel of her tight pussy as it grips me. I let my eyes drift closed. One, two, three pumps and I release into her, pulling back out and tucking myself back inside my pants.

"Always so good. Be a dear and clean yourself up. I've got important things to tend to," I say over my shoulder on my way to the door.

"What sort of things?"

"Well, darling, it's time to prepare for battle."

"Wait, no, you can't!" She moves across the room faster than I thought her capable of and grips my hand tightly in her own.

"I assure you, I can do whatever I please, and what *exactly* are you going to do to stop me? It would be a shame if the other side were to find out you and your brothers have infiltrated their kingdom, wouldn't it?"

She releases my hand, and I ignore the tears pooling in her eyes as I turn away.

The door latches shut behind me and I move down the hall toward where I know Hook is waiting with my men.

CHAPTER 4

Die Trying

PETER

While fucking with people is one of my favorite pastimes, especially when it comes to keeping Wendy and Hook apart, I must follow the instructions in the letter.

I look up from the blade I've been playing with. "Have the men come to the castle."

"You want us to leave the water unattended? Wouldn't that raise alarm for the other side?" Hook asks, his brown eyebrows raised in surprise.

My chair tips as I lean back, placing both feet on the table we're gathered around. "Perhaps. But I'll need all the men to carry the materials for crafting weapons down to the water."

He leans in toward me, hand supporting his weight on the table. "Why the fuck would you want to taunt them?"

"It's simple"—I stand and lean forward, face to face with the hook-handed bastard I've been strapped with all these years—"they've always underestimated me, and I think it's about time I prove them wrong or die trying."

He nods once before drawing himself to his full height and leaving the room to carry out my orders.

"As for the rest of you, I want you to remember that I've protected you and your families all these years from the monsters that roam on the other side."

"But, sir, we've only ever seen one shape-shifter in the forest. Are you sure they're everything you say they are?" one man asks.

"When you've been here as long as I have, you'll see more of their tricks. But truly, I hope we can have them all taken care of by then." My eyes meet those of each man around the table. Most of them nod in agreement before they slowly file out of the room.

CHAPTER 5

Heart With Your Name On It

WENDY

I stand just outside the door when Hook comes out of the room. Quickly, I grasp his hand and pull him down the nearest hallway.

"What's he planning?"

"It's Peter. He's going for maximum damage, or stupidity, whichever way you want to look at it."

The sound of approaching footsteps silences our words. Hook presses me into the wall, hiding me from anyone who might look this way. This was stupid. I should have waited to ask him. I was just so curious about what Peter's planning.

I inhale deeply, appreciating the smell that just *is* Hook.

"Why do you let him treat you that way?" he asks.

"What way?" I snap.

He leans in, his mouth just a breath away from my ear. "You know what I'm talking about."

I bite my lip before responding quietly, "It's not like I have a lot of choice. You know how he is... threatening to tell the king about my brothers spying on his kingdom for as long as we've been here."

He grips my hand and pulls it to his chest before saying, "Well, just so you know, there's a heart with your name on it waiting for you whenever you're ready to defy him." Then, he releases my hand and quickly disappears around the corner.

I bring the hand to my chest and hold it there as a memory comes to the surface.

"Mum, the neighbor boy, Jimmy, said he would walk with me to school. Can I go? Please?"

"Wendy, I don't know this boy. We just got here. I will walk with you."

"But Muuuuummmmm he says he's been walking by himself since he was five. Five! And I'm already eight! Can I please walk with him, please please please," I beg.

She stands looking at me for what feels like forever when a knock sounds at the door. Mum quickly opens it and says, "You must be Jimmy."

From the other side of the door, all I can do is listen and hope she agrees to let me go with him.

"Yes, ma'am, I'm here to walk Wendy to school, if that's okay with you, of course."

I stare at her face and try to force my thoughts into her head. Say yes, say yes, say yes, I repeat.

"I'm going to say yes today, young man. But I expect you to be on your best behavior and bring her back as soon as school is over."

"Yes, ma'am, cross my heart. We'll be home just as quick as can be."

"Thank you, thank you, thank you!" I shout and wrap my arms around Mummy's waist.

"You heard me, Wendy. Straight home after school. I need you to watch your brothers while I get some groceries."

"Yes, ma'am." Quickly, before she can change her mind, I grab my slate and follow Jimmy out the door.

· · ·

My breathing has calmed and I look both ways before leaving the hallway we were tucked in.

Nicole is waiting in our bedchambers when I enter several hours later.

"There you are, God, Wendy, how was it? Tell me everything!"

"Nothing like I expected," I reply.

"When do you have to go back?"

"I'm not sure. As soon as Peter tells me to, I suppose."

She bites her lip while she looks at me, her usual tell that she has something to say and she doesn't know how to get it out.

"Just tell me, Nicole. You're making me nervous."

"I overheard Lucia in the kitchen talking about being with Peter while you were gone..." I'm not surprised by what she says. I'm also not surprised by the fact Lucia was blabbing about it without making sure she wasn't being overheard.

"Lucia says a lot of things."

Her eyes meet mine, and I patiently wait for her to spit it out.

"I saw them... accidentally, of course." She shudders before continuing. "Jesus Christ, I hope I never have to hear Lucia come ever again."

This gets my attention. Peter has never, not in all the times he's blackmailed me to blow him, to pleasure him, or to lie there while he grunts above me, has he ever done anything to make sure that I am left in the same satisfied state.

"I could have lived my entire life without knowing that. Thanks, Nicole." I roll my eyes and laugh it off.

"You're telling me. Unfortunately, the sound has been seared into my brain for all eternity. Ugh."

"I missed you, you know." I pull her to me and hug her.

A knock on the door interrupts our reunion, and I move to answer.

"You have to come with me. I'm afraid he's going to do something really stupid," Hook says and extends his hand to me.

Briefly, I glance back at Nicole before placing my hand in his and following him down the hallway.

Over the next couple of days, Hook and I spend much of our time trying to convince Peter not to do this. But Peter always gets what Peter wants. Or what Tink's letters tell him to do.

"Peter, you're not thinking clearly! Your little Tinkerbell causes chaos. What happens when the other side decides to fight back, huh? Do you have a plan for when they are suddenly on our doorstep?" My nostrils flare. I hate Tinkerbell. She's always sticking her nose where it doesn't belong and Peter always falls for her antics like he's... well, like he's in love with her. And truly, I'd much prefer him to go be with her instead of continuing to blackmail me into being his whore.

He crosses the room in just a few strides, and I back away from him. The look in his eyes tells me I've gone too far. He's angry and I don't know if there's anything I can do to avoid whatever fucked-up response he's going to have.

When my back hits the wall, I know I've only got a few seconds before he's on me.

"Really Peter? Can't even keep your cool for five seconds, can you? No wonder your mother never came looking for you," Hook says from across the room. My eyes fly to him at the same time Peter's entire body shifts toward him before he stomps to the door and slams it behind him.

I clutch my chest, incredibly grateful to have been saved from whatever Peter was about to do to me.

"Thank you," I rasp out.

Hook nods to me and leaves the room.

Most days, I just wish we could go back home. I miss the people we were forced to leave behind because Peter got us all banished.

I miss having the freedom to do what I want.

To be with who I want.

I miss having freedom.

CHAPTER 6

Resolve to Fight

PETER

Hook and Wendy enter the room, and I sigh, rolling my eyes at their sudden camaraderie. My life was so much easier before those two decided to team up. Again.

"Now that you've got all the wood, metal, and other supplies loaded and ready to go, I want you to go back to the water's edge and start making weapons."

The men all watch as Hook and Wendy make their way across the room to stand at my side.

"Are you sure you want to show your hand to the king?" Hook asks. I glare at him. Thankfully, the fucker is smart enough to shut his goddamn mouth.

"Well, I've got to show them something. They need to know that we will do whatever we need to do to protect our children from their shape-shifting, cannibalistic ways." As I look around the room, several of the men nod their agreement at the façade I've worked hard to implant in their stupid brains.

"That'll be all, gentleman," I say, dismissing the rest of them. Hook and Wendy stay behind. The men are smart enough to leave as quickly as they can.

Wendy bites her lip and I know she's about to speak.

I hold up my hand before she has a chance to say anything. "I'm not taking directions from you two. I am resolved to fight. That's the end of it. Wendy, I need to speak with you. In private." I glare at Hook until he rolls his eyes and hesitates before leaving the room.

"Yes?" She meets my gaze and I see something I can't decipher in her eyes today. We'll fix that real damn fast.

It takes three steps before I'm standing directly in front of her. Her eyes fall to my shoes and I grasp her chin, forcing her to look into my eyes again.

"There will be no more spending time with Hook. Do you understand me?" I dig my fingers in a little more, not so patiently waiting for her response.

Instead of agreeing, she purses her lips, and my nostrils flare.

It seems *my* Wendy Darling has acquired a backbone in the last couple of days.

My cock swells and throbs at this little bit of defiance, knowing that I will soon get to have my way with her, to try to break her from this little freedom she thinks she gained in the few weeks she was living in the enemy castle.

"It seems you've excited someone." I pointedly look down at my growing erection. I grasp her shoulders and turn her around, forcing her to lead the way to my room. My hands tightly grip her shoulders the entire way.

"I have a question first..." she trails off. Her backbone seemingly lost in nerves now. We haven't even gotten started yet.

"Pray tell, what could *you* possibly have to ask *me*?" I grasp the collar of my shirt and pull it over my head, tossing it aside.

"Did you sleep with Lucia while I was gone?"

I wonder how she could possibly know this.

"You were gone a long time, Wendy. Surely you didn't think I'd just be pining away for you?" Really, all my cock needs is a warm body. Lucia was a delightful distraction from Wendy's usually unenthusiastic efforts.

She takes a deep breath in before exhaling slowly. "Why don't you ask her to help with your little *problem*?" She spits the word out like somehow my erect cock has deeply offended her.

I chuckle as I answer, "And deprive you of my glorious skills in bed? Never."

With both hands on her waist, I force her up onto the bed. It only takes me a moment to drag her skirts up her legs and plunge myself balls-deep into her tight cunt.

Wendy may not be a completely willing participant, but all these years of blackmail fucks are really starting to grate on me. Lucia has some skills Wendy doesn't.

That Lucia has slept her way around the men in my castle did not go unnoticed by me. I thought it was my turn. Having an opening in my bed seemed like a good time to take the palace whore for a test drive.

I finish, roll off her, and pull my clothes back on. I watch as she pulls her dress back down. When she moves toward the door, I say, "I need you for just one little thing, then you're free to be with whomever you choose."

She stands, hand frozen on the knob. I see her shoulders move up and down as she takes several breaths before responding.

"What would that be?" She doesn't even look at me while she waits for a response. But really, I want to be done with the other king. I want to crush *my* Wendy before tossing her aside, and I couldn't give myself a better Christmas gift.

"I need you to lead the assassination of the king."

She whirls around to face me. "You can't be serious."

In just a few strides, I make it to her, wrap my arm around her waist, and pull her to me. "Oh, I can assure you, I am completely serious." Then press my lips to hers and move around her to leave the room, leaving her to her jumbled thoughts.

Can't Help Myself

WENDY

When I'm finally able to think clearly again, I know I have to leave immediately to head back for Mason's castle.

In a daze, I make my way back to my room where I know Nicole is either reading or napping before her next round of chores. "Wendy? Wendy? Are you okay?" Her voice breaks through my stupor.

"What?"

"I asked if you're okay. You look a little... I'm not sure, but you look strange."

I bark out a laugh. "Well, the king of the pricks just gave me an order that I'm not looking forward to." I sigh and flop down onto the bed.

Nicole marks her place and closes her book before lying down beside me and saying, "I'm sure you'll figure it out, you always do."

"Not this time. He's really trying to fuck me over. I'll be lucky if I make it out of this alive."

She grips my arm. Hard. I wince and pry her fingers off.

"Damn, Nicole, I'd like to keep my hand if there's any chance I will make it through this."

"What is he making you do?"

Mum and Dad are out for the night and I run down the stairs when someone won't stop knocking at the door. I fling the door open and gasp when I see Jimmy standing there, gripping his arm.

"What happened?" I ask.

He keeps his head down and shakes it back and forth. I don't comment on the tear that travels down his nose and falls to his shirt.

"Come in, let me look at that." I reach forward and grasp his hand gently.

"No!" he says as he twists away from me. The look of pain that comes across his face when he jerks his hand away from mine makes me cringe.

I open the door wider, hoping he'll come in. "What happened, Jimmy?" I ask again, hoping he'll trust me this time. This isn't the first time Jimmy's been hurt and won't give an explanation. "We have ice cream. Neapolitan, your favorite!"

For the first time, he looks up at me. His eyes are red all the way around and I hold my breath to keep from crying at the pain I can see in them.

"Your parents won't mind?" he asks so quietly I almost miss it.

Shrugging, I reply, "They won't mind, I promise. It's my tub leftover from my birthday."

Finally, he comes inside and struggles to pull off his coat.

I gasp when I see the bruises already marking his skin. On the top of his forearm, there are four perfectly spaced finger-sized bruises. I can't see the bottom but I would guess that there is one single bruise there marking where a thumb would have been.

"Fell down the steps," he mumbles.

I turn toward the kitchen and discreetly wipe a tear from my cheek.

Jimmy has been my best friend since we moved here five years ago. Mum thinks his dad is the one who hurts him and says that I should be extra nice to him when he's brave enough to come over here after something happens.

After grabbing the ice cream and two spoons, we settle on the couch, the tub between us, and take turns scooping out big spoonfuls of the delicious, cold ice cream.

"Why are you so nice to me?" he asks.

"I just can't help myself."

A knock on my door startles me and I quickly sit back up before Hook strides into the room.

"What are you doing here? You can't just enter a woman's room without her permission. It's not proper!" Nicole says.

I cover my mouth with my hand to hold back a laugh. Because really, so many improper things happen all the time in our castle. Nicole has just never been a part of them.

Hook stands a few steps away from me, pointedly staring at Nicole and then looking at me again.

I hold his gaze as I say, "It's okay, Nicole. I'll see you when I get back again."

"Are you sure? I can stay here if you need me to. It would really be better—"

"I said, I'll see you later. I appreciate your concern."

She hesitates briefly before finally leaving the room.

"What are you doing here?" I ask.

He crosses the remaining distance in long strides and looks down at me, where I still sit on the edge of the bed. His messy brown hair falls across his eye, and I reach up and move it out of the way automatically. He closes his eyes and shudders at the contact.

"Are you okay?" His eyes sweep down my body after he asks.

I raise my chin before replying, "I'm fine."

I don't have a choice. I don't just have myself to think about.

Peter threatens my brothers every chance he gets, and while they may be grown now, as the big sister, I will *always* feel they are my responsibility. So for now, what Peter wants, Peter gets.

I drop my chin to my chest and mumble, "I don't want to do this, but I don't have a choice."

He reaches out and fingers my long brown hair. "Just... be careful, okay?"

"You don't even know what he's asked... what's he's making me do."

"There's always a choice."

My eyes fall to my hands clenched in my lap. "Not for me."

"Your brothers can take care of themselves." He reaches out, and with a gentle grip, lifts my chin so I'm looking into his eyes again. "You have put up with his bullshit for too long. You have protected them for too long. They have to take responsibility for their own willingness to go along with Peter's plans at some point."

I shove him back and stand. "I'm not just going to let him get my brothers killed, Hook. They're the only family I have left."

A tear falls and Hook reaches up to wipe it away before I can stop him. "They don't deserve your loyalty. Fuck, Peter doesn't deserve you either."

"And you think you do? Be serious, Hook, it would never work. We'll never be together. Not as long as we're stuck here." We continue to stare at each other for several seconds before I say, "It's time for you to leave. I need to get my things together."

I give him a single nod and he leaves me to finish gathering my stuff.

"Oh, my God, Wendy. What was that?" Nicole asks, entering the room and moving quickly to me, grasping my hands in hers.

"Just Hook being concerned," I reply as a smile creeps across my face. "I'm going to miss you, you know that?"

"You'll be back before you know it."

As I make my way through the hallways toward the exit, I

can't help but glance around, wondering if I'll ever see this place again. I can't imagine the other side takes assassinations lightly. Fuck, I'll probably be dead soon.

CHAPTER 8

Boy Like Me

HOOK

Ever since I met her, even before I knew what a crush was, I loved Wendy Darling. She sat on the ground playing with her doll and I watched from my yard until I worked up the courage to make my way over to her.

The years passed, and she always treated me like a friend, and I refused to drag her into my fucked-up family. So I did what I needed to do to keep her safe, protect her in the ways I could not protect my mum.

"James! Where the fuck have you run off to?"

We both turn toward my dad, yelling out my front door.

"I've got to go," I say.

"It was nice meeting you."

I watch as her cheeks turn pink, and she continues to watch me walk backward toward my house.

"If you'd like, you can walk with me to school tomorrow. I know the way. I've been walking all by myself since I was five."

"I'll ask my mummy if that would be okay. See you tomorrow then?"

"James, if you're not in this house in the next ten seconds, you know what will happen!" my dad yells, and I cringe inside, knowing what's probably coming.

"Bye, Wendy," I say and immediately turn and run up the steps of my porch and into my house.

"Where have you been? I didn't say you could leave this house!" Dad yells at me as soon as the door closes behind me.

I look around the room, looking for my mum. From the corner I hear her say, "Roy, he was just saying hi to the new neighbors. You don't want them to think we're not neighborly, do you?"

"I'll get to you later," he bites out and grabs my arm.

The next morning, I search through my drawers for a shirt that can cover the bruises left behind on my arm. There is nothing I can do to avoid my bottom hurting when I have to sit in the hard chairs at school today. My mum cried from her spot in the corner when dad bent me over the couch, holding me in place with one arm while he pulled his belt out with the other hand.

When I go into her room to say goodbye, she is covering up her own bruises with makeup.

"I'm sorry I wasn't here sooner, Mummy. I didn't see his car pull in."

She turns to me and motions me to her. "You are not the grown-up here, Jimmy, it's my job to protect you." She holds either side of my face and gives me a kiss on the nose. "Dad just had a bad day at work yesterday. He promises he'll do better."

We've heard that excuse so many times, I somehow manage not to roll my eyes. It's not Mum's fault Dad is so mean. "I'll be home just as soon as school is over, okay?"

"I love you. Be safe."

"Love you, too, Mum." I grab my slate before running out the door and walking over to Wendy's house.

I knock on the door and a woman quickly opens it and says, "You must be Jimmy."

My eyes look past her, trying to catch sight of Wendy somewhere in the house. This must be her mum. She looks nice.

"Yes, ma'am, I'm here to walk Wendy to school, if that's okay with you, of course."

I stare into her face and wait for her reply.

"I'm going to say yes today, young man. But I expect you to be on your best behavior and bring her back as soon as school is over."

"Yes, ma'am, cross my heart. We'll be home just as quick as can be." Which works since I already promised my mum I would be home then, too.

"Thank you, thank you, thank you!" I hear from behind the door and then I see Wendy wrap her arms around her mum's waist.

"You heard me, Wendy. Straight home after school. I need you to watch your brothers while I get some groceries."

"Yes, ma'am." A second later, Wendy comes bounding out the door holding her slate.

"All ready?"

"Yep!" She winds her arm through mine and I flinch when her hand grazes my bruises. "Are you okay?"

I take a few deep breaths before replying, "I'm fine." Then lead the way to school.

Dad got drunk tonight. Then when I got home from school, I forgot to set my shoes to the side when I took them off, just the way Dad likes it. He called me to him in a weirdly nice voice.

As soon as I saw my shoes on the floor, I tried to run away. Instead, he picked them up and hurled them at me across the living *room. Thankfully, Mum is still at her sister's house helping with the new baby.*

I'm a man now, I can take it, and the punishment continues until finally he passes out in an alcohol-induced sleep. The road feels too wide as I make my way across it to Wendy's house.

I continue knocking at the door, waiting for someone to answer. The front porch light is off and their car is gone, but I hope that someone, anyone, *is home. The door flings open and Wendy gasps when she sees me standing here, gripping my arm.*

"What happened?" she asks.

I keep my head down and shake it back and forth. She doesn't comment on the tear that I can't stop from traveling down my nose and falling to my shirt.

"Come in, let me look at that." She reaches forward and grasps my hand gently.

"No!" I yell as I twist away from her. She cringes when I can't keep my carefully crafted mask in place.

She opens the door wider, inviting me in. "What happened, Jimmy?" she asks again, hoping I'll give her some kind of answer this time. This isn't the first time I've been hurt and have refused to give an explanation. "We have ice cream, Neapolitan, your favorite!"

For the first time, I look up at her. She bites her lip and holds her breath when she gets a look at my face. I look back down at the ground, avoiding her gaze again.

"Your parents won't mind?" I ask quietly.

She shrugs when she replies, "They won't mind, I promise. It's my tub leftover from my birthday."

Finally, I go inside and then struggle to pull off my coat.

The bruises are already marking my skin. It didn't cross my mind to change into a fresh shirt to cover everything up. Hide it away so that Wendy doesn't feel sorry for me.

"Fell down the steps," I mumble.

I don't miss the tear that she wipes away.

Wendy has been my refuge since she moved here with her

family. I'm pretty sure her parents know that it's my dad hurting me. They've never said anything to me, though.

Wendy grabs ice cream and two spoons, we sit on the couch, the tub between us, and take turns taking big spoonfuls and shoving them into our mouths.

With bellies full, we lie back on the couch, our heads together and legs draped over the arms. "How can I help you, Jimmy?"

"Just help me forget."

Wendy jumps into the same story she always tells me on nights like this. She paints pictures with her words about the island. Neverland is an imaginary island where nothing bad happens and you can escape all the bad things in life.

At eight years old, Wendy was there for me after one of the first beatings Dad ever gave me. He told me then that I was now old enough to be punished like a man.

While she continues to tell the story of the make-believe place of our dreams, I know that she'll never want to be with a boy like me. Her life is sunshine and rainbows. She spends her days teaching her brothers and helping her mum bake. I spend my days trying not to do anything to make my dad mad. If everything is perfect, he won't have anything to hit me for, right?

One good thing about growing up is he no longer takes it out on my mum. He reserves everything for me. That's the only thing I'll be grateful for. I can now protect my mum.

Tears slide down my cheeks and I let them fall, listening to Wendy's calming cadence.

CHAPTER 9

The Takeover

WENDY

I don't want to do this.

I don't want to do this.

I don't want to do this.

I make my way to the outdoor door and let in some of Peter's men, then lead them through Mason's castle. Thankfully, they were camped nearby and saw my signal quickly. We stay quiet, not wanting to draw any attention to ourselves as we prepare for what Peter is forcing me to execute.

Patiently, we wait outside the room. I saw them all enter it a short time ago. I've been sneaking around, monitoring everyone for days. It's only now that the opportunity has presented itself.

I hold my breath as we hear the handle on the door jiggle. It's time for the takeover. One of the idiots Peter sent drops his damn arrow and makes an insane amount of noise in the quiet hallway. Thug number two releases the tension on his own bow and punches him in the arm.

He finally recovers himself as the door cracks open. I watch as he nocks the arrow again and draws the string to his jaw.

The door opens wider and I glance up to see the king standing in the doorway. It didn't take long to come up with a plan. They're supposed to take out the king and then capture Callie and bring her back with them to our castle.

Dumbass releases his arrow too soon and ends up hitting the king in the thigh. Then there's a scramble from inside the room and the door is pulled closed.

"Leave, *now,*" I grind out quietly.

Both men look at me before nodding and gathering their quivers from against the wall behind them and following me out the way we came.

I hold the door open for them before attempting to make my way out of the mountain. Before I'm able to cross through the door, I feel something tug on the back of my dress.

"Not so fast," I hear from the man who's got ahold of me.

One of the idiots turns around to see what's holding me up.

"Run!" I shout, and he quickly regains himself and disappears into the trees.

"We're just going to take you down to the cells and see what we can find out about this assassination attempt on the king."

"I don't know what you're talking about." I hold my chin high, defiance in my gaze.

"I'm not falling for your innocent little girl act. You're coming with me."

He motions to another man, who grabs a torch before coming with us down one of the lesser-used passages.

They stay silent while we move down the long tunnel. It's almost a straight shot further underground to where they have the cells for prisoners.

This part of the castle was not on my brief tour they gave me when I started working here. Since most people in this world are not stupid enough to attack each other, these cells have probably never been used.

One man unlocks the cell before the one holding my arms shoves me inside and the door is locked again.

"What? You're just going to leave me here?" I call after them.

The room grows darker as the sound of their footsteps fades in the distance, along with the light from the torch.

Both hands grip the bars. I didn't get a good look around the cell before being plunged into darkness. I'd really rather not injure myself in here, so I wait patiently, knowing at some point, they have to send someone in to interrogate me.

CHAPTER 10

Down

WENDY

It's *hours* before anyone comes back to talk to me. At some point I start nervously pacing the small cell waiting, hoping, praying that the king survived. I know everything will be much worse for me if he bleeds to death from the leg wound.

The plan was most definitely *not* for one of us to get caught. But in the back of my head, I knew it was a possibility. It's not like they leave themselves susceptible to attack.

While I wait, I remember a story I once told to a little boy so long ago to take his mind off of the bad things that happened to him.

"There once was an island called... it was called Neverland. Where kids could go and never grow up. On this island there was a... there was a... crocodile! That's it. There was a crocodile. And he loved to spend his days swimming through the water. Occasionally, he would pick on his favorite pirate, Captain Hook."

"Pirates? I thought you said the kids never grew up?" Jimmy interrupts.

"Jimmy, I said they could go and never grow up. I didn't say they stayed young forever without choice."

"Sorry, sorry, continue your story."

Jimmy sits on his hands like that will keep him from interrupting me.

Slowly, down the tunnel, I see a light grow closer, brighter, and as soon as the torch has made its way into the room, I see Theodore. He places the torch in one of the wall sconces and crosses his arms, leaning against the wall across from me. He doesn't speak, just watches me for several minutes.

I know I'm more likely to incriminate myself if I speak, so I stare right back at him.

It somehow feels like it takes forever and also not nearly long enough when he finally speaks. The sudden sound in the silence startles me.

"I will not pretend I'm not disappointed in your actions tonight. But mostly, I'm disappointed in myself. I brought you into the castle. I watched you. I questioned you. And I approved you to work here. What was the plan tonight?"

I bite my lips to keep from saying anything. Especially something that could make this worse for me. I'd like to think that they can't break me. That they can't take me down. But I also know that it would have been smarter for Peter to have done this himself, or to have sent Hook in my stead.

Now I'm here, alone.

Unlike the two of them, I'm more likely to tell all our secrets.

"So it's going to be that way, then? That's fine. You'll talk. Eventually." He slides down the wall to sit on the floor, legs in front of him crossed at the ankle.

It grows increasingly awkward in the silence, and eventually, I make my way over to the rickety bed and sit down. My eyes are on Theodore the entire time.

Some time later, another man enters and hands him a pouch.

Theodore thanks him and pulls a small table from the side of the room, slowly unrolling the bundle and revealing its contents.

"I thought we would start with something small. I'm particularly fond of this." He twirls one of the weapons in his hand and I recognize it as something Peter's used before to torture answers out of people.

I shudder at the memory and scoot back on the thin mattress, tucking my legs up against me and wrapping my arms around them.

He comes to the bars and squats down to be at my eye level again. "Do I need to use these, or will you tell me what I want to know?"

I bite my lips again, hesitating. If it gets back to Peter that I cooperated, I know it will be worse for me over on his side of the water. But right now, Theodore is extending an olive branch, and I have to do what I have to do to stay alive.

CHAPTER 11

F**k It

WENDY

I lick my lips before replying, "What do you want to know?"

I refuse to give away any more information than I need to. There are people on the other side I love dearly and I would hate to rain down any kind of punishment they don't deserve.

"Why? Why did you plan an attack on the king?"

"Because I was ordered to." I'll give the shortest answers I can for as long as he'll let me.

"By who?" He comes closer to the bars, and his arm holding the tool falls to his side. His other hand grasps one of the bars and he presses himself against them.

I stay on the bed. While the mattress is uncomfortable, I have no desire to put myself within reach of that thing if I can help it. I've seen grown men reduced to tears when Peter has used things like that. He's fond of the more violent ways of acquiring information.

"Someone I'm more scared of than your little tools over there." I jerk my chin toward his table of torture devices.

A smile spreads across his face. "You've seen things like this before?" he asks, raising his hand holding the small tool.

I nod once in response. Given the option, Peter would choose torture as his preferred method of acquiring information every time. What happened to him as a child to make him the way he is, we will probably never know. What we do know is, he is one fucked-up son of a bitch.

"So this person you're more scared of than me. Do they have a name?"

I purse my lips, knowing that if I give them an answer, if it got back to Peter that I cooperated with them, I'd be dead.

"It's going to be that way, huh? Why don't we start with where you came here from?"

Instead of answering, I pull my long brown hair over my shoulder and braid it. When I've secured the end, I look back up and he watches me, patiently waiting for my response.

"Every time you've been brought here, Joe and Ralph have accompanied you. How do you know them?" He places the tool in his hand down and picks up something I've never seen before. The end of it is pointy, and he pricks the tip of his finger, a drop of blood instantly coming to the surface. "This one is particularly effective. You place the point under the fingernail, like so..." He demonstrates on his own hand, not pushing it in enough to draw blood this time.

"Maybe we should send a messenger to bring them here. Maybe they would be willing to answer my quest—"

"*No!*" It flies from my mouth and I bite my lips to keep from saying more.

"So you do know them... interesting." He places the tool back with the rest and returns to his place on the floor, legs crossed in front of him. "Tell you what, if you answer some of my questions, I'll leave them alone. They're related to you... yes?"

My eyes grow wide and a smile crosses his face at my obvious admission.

"What do you want from me?" I ask in defeat. My hands grip the edge of the bed and I lean forward, giving him my full attention.

"In exchange for your help in gathering information, we are prepared to offer you full protection, along with Joe and Ralph, if you so wish."

I stand, making my way to the bars and gripping them so tightly my knuckles turn white. "Swear it, swear you'll protect them."

"I swear to you, I will do everything in my power to keep them safe."

Fuck it, I'm tired of playing Peter's games. It's time I take my future into my own hands.

"Oh, my God, Wendy! You have to tell me what happened!" Nicole says as soon as I get to my room in Peter's castle.

"Shhhhh, be quiet." I move across the room to her and pull her into my arms. "What are you doing in here, anyway?"

She shrugs as she says, "I saw the wagon coming and figured I'd just wait for you here."

"Let's just hope no one else saw me coming," I mutter.

"Did you really do it? Did you assassinate the king?"

My eyes fly to hers. "How did you even know about that?"

"Word travels fast around here, Wendy. And Peter is an over-confident asshole." She moves to my chest and starts to unpack my belongings.

"Where's Hook?" I ask.

Nicole bites her lip, continuing to put my things back where they belong and making a small pile of the things she deems as needing to be cleaned.

"Nicole... what are you not telling me?"

"He's not here, okay? Peter sent him off on some scouting excursion."

Thankful for the bed behind me as I lose all strength in my legs, I collapse back onto the edge. "What has he done?" My eyes raise to see her watching me curiously, frozen in place with one of my dresses in her grasp.

CHAPTER 12

All About Me

WENDY

I pace back and forth in my room, wracking my brain about what I can do. The reason he banished Hook does not escape me. He knows. He's probably always known. On top of everything else, I'm pissed I missed spending Christmas with Nicole and everyone else.

Today I am feeling grown up. Mum finally let me wear a longer dress. It took me extra long to do my hair this morning. New clothes, new hairstyle.

When I walk out of my bedroom, Mum covers her mouth and I see tears welling in her eyes.

"What is it? Is something wrong with the way I look?" I slowly twirl so she can see all the way around.

"You just look so... grownup. I want you to remember your manners at school today. You know the rules, straight home after class. Make sure your brothers do the same," she tells me before pulling me in for a hug.

Michael comes running through the hall, shoes that look too big for him clutched in his child-sized hands.

"Michael! You come back here right now with my shoes or we're gonna be late for school!" John follows closely behind.

"Boys, you behave for your sister."

They both stop and turn toward my dad, who stands at the bottom of the stairs.

"Yes, Dad," they reply.

When they've both finally gotten ready, we leave for the short trek to school. Jimmy waits for us on our porch and we all walk together.

It's been so long since someone new has come here that I'm surprised when there's a boy I don't recognize in class. Several times I catch him looking at me across the room and I keep my head down to focus on my work.

When we gather our things to leave, I hear, "Hey, Wendy!" The voice is unfamiliar and I pause a second to look at Jimmy before I turn around.

The boy stands a few steps away, and he watches me curiously, hands in his pockets.

"Yes?" I ask as I wrap my scarf around my neck.

"I wanted to know if you wanted to hang out with me?"

I look at this strange boy and wonder, why me? "Can't. I told my mum I'd come home right after school. Maybe some other time?"

He nods and I turn to grab my stuff off the bench, but it's not there. Jimmy holds it up and smiles at me before opening the door and motioning me through.

It doesn't go unnoticed by me that he glances back one last time and smirks at the new boy before closing the door behind him and walking with us back home.

The only reason I even put up with Peter is because of how he is. Controlling. Domineering. A complete and utter prick.

I curl my fingers around my thumb into a fist and punch the wall as hard as I can. The snap I feel jolts me out of my angry haze and the pain focuses everything to that point on my hand. My injured hand pressed to my chest, I use the other hand to yank the door open and immediately take a step back when I see him standing in the doorway.

"What do you want?" I spit.

That sadistic grin comes to his face before his eyes drop to the awkward way I hold my hand against me.

"What happened to you?" Peter asks, his hand darting out, gripping my wrist painfully and pulling it toward him. "You know you're supposed to keep your thumb on the outside, right?"

I don't dare yank away from him, afraid he'd lash out and probably cause further injury. Or just keep me away from the healers for longer.

"You should really get that taken care of." He releases my hand and steps back out of the doorway.

The door clicks closed behind me and I don't look back to see if he follows as I make my way to the healer's hall.

When I enter the room, several people turn to look at me. "I need help. I've injured my hand."

A woman makes her way to me and reaches her hand out, palm up and flat. She motions with her fingers for me to allow her to inspect my hand.

Slowly, carefully, I move my hand away from my chest and place it in her upturned palm. She gently moves it from side to side, inspecting the injury. Over her shoulder, I see a man approaching. He watches my hand as she moves it back and forth before he moves away and returns with a couple of jars and some bandages.

They bring me to one of the beds around the perimeter of the room and motion for me to sit on the end.

Few words are said as they realign my thumb, apply some salves, and splint and wrap everything up to help it stay immobile.

As soon as I enter my room, Nicole waits for me and immediately looks down at my hand.

"What happened to you?" she asks.

I move toward where she sits on the edge of the bed and flop backward onto its soft surface. "I punched the wall."

"You... punched the wall? You know you're supposed to keep your thumb on the outside, right?"

My eyes dart to her, and she bites her lip. "So I've been told."

"Well, I thought you might be interested to know the kitchen staff has been exceedingly busy while you've been off having your wounds tended to."

I sit up at her words, sure that she'll eventually get to the point. When she stays silent, looking at me pointedly, I decide to ask, "And?"

"Well, aren't you just a bundle of sunshine today? I've never seen them prepare so much food, even when everyone has been in our castle at once. You and I both know that the castle has not been full for quite some time. So you might ask yourself, why has Peter ordered the kitchens to prepare all the food and pack it away?"

I use my good hand to help me back off of the bed. Nicole's eyes follow me as I pace back and forth in my room for the second time today. "What is that little bastard up to?"

Our heads both turn toward the door when someone raps once on the hard surface before opening it. In the doorway stands Peter.

"Oh good, you're both here. Wendy, I came in here earlier to let you know you need to pack your things. Pack light, we've got a ways to travel. With your little accident, I'm sure Nicole is free to help you gather what you'll need for the trip."

He turns on his heel and leaves without so much as a backward glance to make sure we follow orders.

I'm done catering to his every whim. As soon as I can figure out how to get rid of Peter, it's all about me.

PART FOUR

I Told You War Was a Bad Idea

CHAPTER 13

It's a War

PETER

"Oh good, you're just in time," I say when Wendy walks into the room where I'm giving everyone instructions.

She looks around at all the men in the room and stands against the wall near the door. I'm certain she's just making sure she can leave as quickly as possible.

"It's time. It's time to pack everything up and head off to the tunnels. Stay out of sight of the other castle. You should be able to get the women, children, and elderly in and settled before night-fall." I nod to the group in charge of moving people and provisions into the tunnels Hook has been busy preparing and they exit the room.

To the remaining men, I order, "The rest of you, I want to start this off with a *bang*. Load the cannons on their wagons and take them through the trees, but only so far as you can travel without being spotted. I want you to roll them the rest of the way and aim for the side of the mounta—"

"*No!*"

My head swings toward the door, nostrils flared as I glare at Wendy.

Her hand covers her mouth and her eyes are wide as she realizes that she's going to pay for speaking against me in front of my men.

"As I was saying, aim for the side of the mountain. The rest of you I want hidden in the trees on either side of their entrance, ready and waiting for them to assemble their men before attacking. I've got some surprises up my sleeve and I want them distracted. Do you understand your orders?"

My gaze moves around the room and I meet the eyes of each man in command of my men. When the last man has met my eyes and nodded his head, I dismiss them before turning on Wendy.

"You've been a very bad girl, Wendy." Stalking toward her, I grasp her good wrist tightly in my hand before pulling her against me.

We're about to carry out the plans from Tink's letter and my cock is hard as a rock just thinking about the look on their king's face when he realizes that his new pet is missing.

"No, not today. I'm done. You said as soon as I led the assassination of the king, you would let me be with whomever I wanted to be."

Grasping her chin roughly, I bite out, "And yet, he's not dead now, is he?" One arm wrapped around her, the other hand still gripping her face, I silently demand she kisses me, forcing my tongue past her lips. I spin us and lead her back toward the table all the plans are laid out on.

When she tries to resist me, I use force to lay her back on the surface. "You will give in to this, because you know it could be so much worse... for you. It's a war, Wendy. What did you think was going to happen?"

She stops fighting me and I pull up her skirt with one hand while unfastening my pants with the other.

The door slams open behind me, interrupting my entertainment.

"What are you doing?" comes from behind me and I smirk, recognizing Hook's voice immediately.

Unfortunately, that voice has an immediate effect on my dick, and it deflates in seconds. I tuck myself back into my pants before shoving past him and out to the waiting wagons.

CHAPTER 14

Desire Into Gold

PETER

It takes hours before the wagon I ride alongside arrives at the tree line. I jump down and move between the trees. Wendy and Hook will be waiting for me as soon as I make it to the tunnels.

I watch as, across the clearing, my men load the cannons. When they fire them toward the mountain, some rock is knocked loose and we all stay in the trees waiting for them to leave the protection of the mountain like ants.

At the first sign of someone exiting, I mount my horse and stay low to his back as we ride as fast as he will move through the forest to the tunnel entrance. Hook greets me as soon as I've handed off my horse.

"Where's Wendy?" are the first words out of my mouth.

He clenches his jaw at my words before responding, "She and Nicole are helping get everyone settled."

My shoulder knocks into his as I shove past him and make my way down the dimly lit tunnel. From the doorway, I watch as she moves back and forth, passing out food and other supplies to people, keeping her injured hand protected. Such a rookie mistake to punch with your thumb inside your fist. When she notices me, she stiffens before continuing what she was doing.

The next time I'm able to catch her eye, I jerk my chin at a side tunnel. For far too long, I wait. And wait. And wait. Before finally exiting the tunnel to see where she's run off to.

Wendy is nowhere to be seen, and I make my way over to where Hook leans against the wall with a smirk on his face.

"What have you done with her?" I grind out through clenched teeth.

"What have I done with whom?" he responds.

He doubles over as my fist connects with his abdomen. I lean in close, hunching over his frame. "You will pay for this. I know what you two are doing and I think it's about time you remember that *I* am the one in charge around here."

CHAPTER 15

Race You to the Bottom

HOOK

I don't dare let Peter leave my sight. Wendy and Nicole are off together in one of the tunnel branches, hiding from him.

His actions have grown progressively erratic and I fear what he might make Wendy do.

When Michael and John enter a short time later, I make my way over to where they all stand. "Where have you two been?" I ask.

They exchange glances with Peter before he speaks up. "They've been working on a little... project for me. I'd like you to go take care of that as a way to stay in my good graces, of course."

He jerks his chin for me to follow Wendy's brothers and I roll my eyes when I turn. I'm surprised that he follows us out. We stop at an empty tunnel and I hear the soft cries of what sounds like a feminine voice.

I glance at Peter and ask, "Who's in there?"

"The king's whore. She also happens to be the newest resident of our world," he replies.

Peter waits at the entrance. I follow the brothers, and the only light source in the dark tunnel, to one of the small rooms off the corridor. They motion me to enter first. Arms crossed, hook gleaming in the torchlight, I enter the cavern. I only allow myself a second to take in the scene before advancing, knowing Peter is watching from the shadows to see if I'll follow his command.

The woman's lips are pinched together when I enter and say, "Something amusing to you?" I watch the light die in her eyes before continuing, "It seems we have a bit of a problem. You see, your king has taken something that does not belong to him."

Though the room is dimly lit, I watch a tremor shake her body as I circle around her. "Really? What's that?" she asks.

I stop in front of her and reply, "You." Then reach out and grasp her chin. This one has some fight to her, and I smirk as she tries to pull away from me.

"And why would you think I belong to you?" she asks.

"You see, we have a little, silent treaty of sorts..." I trail off as I think about what lie I want to tell her. I'm pulling this out of my ass as I go. "Every time a new prisoner comes here, we have always divided the captives evenly. But you see, you were to be our captive. It was our turn, and I heard through the... grapevine that there was a new person here. And to my surprise, I found out the rumors were true when you were spotted wandering among the villagers."

Grapevine, Wendy, her idiot brothers, who's to say where the rumors originated. It wasn't me.

"There seems to be a teeny tiny problem with your 'silent treaty.'"

I quirk an eyebrow at her comment. "Oh really? And what's that?" I lean forward in an attempt to intimidate her. Unfortunately, leaning in close to her, I don't realize what she's about to do until it's too late. Her knee slams into my groin and all the air leaves my lungs.

The back of my hand connects with her cheek and the spit flies from her mouth as her head jerks to the side. Once I can stand straight again, I spit in her face, before landing the first shot to her body.

With the brothers in the room, I know I have to make some kind of show of strength or they'll tell Peter I took it easy on her. I shudder to think what he would do to her if she went unpunished. Keeping my hook away from her, I land several more shots to her, avoiding any areas that would cause serious injury.

Turning on my heel, I leave the cavern, and the brothers follow me out. I fight the urge to vomit as visions of my father's abuse flash through my mind.

Peter moves to speak, and I shove past him. "Did you work out all of your aggression? Really, it was about time you had a little fun. You've gotten increasingly tense as of late. What's wrong, Hook, can't get any pussy these days?"

Before my brain registers what's happening, my hand fists his shirt and I have him pressed against the wall. "You really should learn to keep your fucking mouth shut. I'm not afraid to race you to the bottom, but I will scratch, claw, and climb my way back out to be with her. And if you think you can stand between us forever, you're wrong. I'm just waiting for the day you fuck up so bad, that she decides her brothers can take care of themselves."

In my peripheral, I see both of them stiffen, probably deciding the likelihood of Peter turning them over to the king on the other side.

His mouth quirks up and he shoves me back. "Oh, Hook, I have another task for you. It seems we've been given another little visitor, and I need you to make sure she stays alive."

"Seems to me she's *your* little visitor. What makes you think I want to make her *my* problem?"

"If you scratch my back, I'll scratch yours, or some shit like that." He moves past me and I watch him disappear down the tunnel. "John can show you where to find her. I expect her to be alive when they come back for her."

Michael and Peter disappear down the tunnel and I glance at John before he leads me a short distance to another cavern.

CHAPTER 16

Dangerous

PETER

Sometime later, I send Michael off on some errand. Really, I just wanted him to stop talking to me like we were friends or some shit.

Quietly, I make my way down the tunnel before finally entering the cavern. "Oh dear, look at what a mess you are. Here, let me help you," I say.

Against the wall are a couple of chairs and I grab one before bringing it behind her. I know the second I lower her arms, she'll collapse, so I position the chair just behind her legs so she has somewhere to land other than the floor.

Not wanting to give her too much freedom, I leave her still chained, but I do give her some small slack in the chain so she can regain some of the feeling in her arms. The tears that flow down her cheeks with the relief brings me a sense of accomplishment.

I grab a second chair from the wall and sit across from her. "I'm truly sorry for the way my people have treated you. I assure you, I was unaware of the depth of their depravity, my dear." The lie falls from my lips easily, because of course I am the one who sent them all here to abuse her.

She purses her lips and I know that I have failed to hide the malice in my tone. I motion for her to give me her hands, and she tucks them against herself.

"You're a stubborn one, aren't you?"

I laugh when she gives me an angry look.

"Perhaps I should introduce myself. My name is Peter." I hold out my hand to see if she'll willingly shake hands with me. When she refuses to give me her hand, I quickly reach forward and snatch both hands, yanking them toward me. "Really, what could your king have expected? You belong to me."

"I belong to no one," she growls. Really, the fact that she even has any fight left amuses me. We did kidnap her right out from under their noses.

"I assure you, my dear, you *will* tell me what I want to know, or you will not like the consequences." I bring her hand to my lips and kiss the back of it.

As soon as I pull back, she spits on me. My vision turns red, anger that this little bitch thinks she can just disrespect me like this in *my* place. She doesn't know just how dangerous I can be. Abruptly, I stand, grabbing my chair and throwing it across the room. "You really shouldn't have done that," I roar, and move swiftly back to the wall, pulling her chain fast.

This time, I don't want her to have any ability to rest and I continue to tug on the chain until she's standing on her toes. It doesn't take me long to secure the chain to it before quickly leaving the room.

When I make it back to the room where everyone else waits, my cock is hard and I don't see Wendy anywhere in sight. I motion Hook over to me. "Where are Wendy and her little friend?"

He shrugs and my eyes narrow at the action. I had a feeling he was hiding them from me when they were missing earlier. His evasive behavior now only confirms it.

Lucia catches my eye and I jerk my chin toward one of the

side entrances before waiting for Hook to finish whatever excuse he's making up. She quickly makes her way down the darkened passage, and as soon as Hook shuts the fuck up, I follow, palming my cock through my pants while I make my way down the passage after her.

I'm Taking Things Into My Own Hands

Never Heard

WENDY

"How long do you think we'll have to wait here?" Nicole asks.

We sit on the floor in the torchlight, waiting for Hook to come and tell us the coast is clear.

Over the next couple of weeks, the new boy, Peter, keeps talking to me, trying to get to know me. Jimmy is the only boy besides my brothers I've ever been able to talk to without feeling weird.

Talking to Peter, though, makes my tummy feel funny, like something is flying around in there. He brings me flowers and cookies sometimes.

Jimmy doesn't like Peter though. He keeps telling me to stay away from him. He never gives me a solid reason, though, I like the attention Peter gives me.

In the distance, I hear muffled cries and I stand, grabbing the torch and making my way toward the sound. Nicole follows close behind, gripping my arm above my injured hand.

When we make it to the cavern, I see Callie suspended by a chain. "Oh, my God," I breathe.

Nicole pushes past me and carefully runs her fingers down Callie's face. "What happened to her? Who is this?"

I step forward, bringing the light closer so we can see the damage to her. "We won't be able to get her down ourselves. I have to go. I have to tell them where she is."

"Wait, Wendy, *who is this?*" Nicole repeats and I hand her the torch.

"This is the king's girl, and I know he will move heaven and earth to find her. I'll be back."

"I don't understand? The king..." she trails off before realization lights up her eyes. "You don't mean... you do! Why do you care about the other side's people?"

"He's not what we've been led to believe. He's good, Nicole, so good. And Callie doesn't deserve whatever has happened to her here. Go back to the tunnel we were in before. If Hook or Peter come back, tell them I've gone to the bathroom or something, do *not* tell them where I am."

"Well, that's easy. I don't know where you're going to be."

I pull her close to me before telling her to be careful and feel my way down the dark passageways until I see the sunlight at the end of the tunnel.

I stay hidden in the trees, making my way on foot as quickly as I can. It doesn't take me long to find the search party. His men have been scouring the forest.

When I see Theodore, he immediately leads me to where

Mason is giving orders. He turns at the sound of newcomers and his shoulders fall when he sees me.

"She's dead, isn't she?" he asks.

I move toward him, arm outstretched. "Not yet," I reply. "But you need to come quickly. There's no telling what they'll do to her if she's left there too much longer."

He dismisses everyone but James and Steve, and they follow me through the forest. When we get to the tunnel, I show them to the entrance and tell them where they can find her before ducking down another tunnel to wait for their footsteps to retreat.

It doesn't take them long to get her and leave. I quietly make my way back to where Nicole is supposed to be, only she's not there.

I search down a few more tunnels before carefully making my way back to where everyone else waits.

My heart clenches in my chest when I see Hook talking to her, his eyes frantically flying around the room, I assume, looking for me.

"Wendy, I don't think you should go out with him tonight. Something is weird with him. I just can't put my finger on it," Jimmy says.

"Are you sure it isn't just you're mad you didn't have the idea first?"

He grabs my shoulder and turns me to face him.

John and Michael run ahead, wanting nothing to do with our conversation.

"Do you really think that? Do you really think I'm... what? Jealous or something?"

I shrug and look down at my feet.

"I wish..." He pulls me to him, one arm wrapped around my back, the other hand tangles in my hair.

My arms are dangling by my sides, the shock of our current position stilling any movement. "What are you—"

His lips come to mine, erasing every thought in my head. My hands come up to pull him closer to me, holding him to me as we continue to kiss on the sidewalk.

He moves back and rests his forehead on mine. "You've got me wrong, Wendy. I don't deserve you, and one day I know you'll stop talking to me. But I have to make sure that you hear this. There is something wrong with Peter. Be careful."

"Have you never heard a word I've said? You are not your father. I know you would never hurt me." I tilt my head back up, trying to steal another kiss, but he releases me, pushing me away from him gently.

"Let's go home."

PART SIX

Rash Decisions

CHAPTER 18

Own It

PETER

While the sun is up, I decide to go outside and get some fresh air. The smell is rank in the cave with all the bodies pressed in together and I look forward to being able to move everyone to our new home.

When I pass by the cavern where the king's whore was, I'm surprised to find it empty. I turn away, rage driving me down the tunnel to its entrance.

Fortunately, tracking is something I've done since I was a kid. I squat down and observe the footprints before following their path.

From a distance, I see Jimmy pulling Wendy to him and I watch their mouths moving. Unfortunately, I can't get close enough to hear without them noticing me.

When he kisses her, I grind my teeth together. She. Is. Mine. He needs to keep his damn hands off of her.

I've been slowly incorporating myself into her life, trying to get her to let her guard down so I can get her alone and show her how she really makes me feel.

This is just a minor inconvenience for my plans. I'll just have to work extra hard to convince her I'm a good guy. Ha. What a fucking joke.

When I hear voices, I slow my approach, quieting my footsteps so I don't alert anyone. They've set up a campsite and I duck down and watch the various people move back and forth throughout the area.

In the biggest tent, I hear two people speaking in hushed voices and I carefully move toward it. I hear an older woman speaking with a man about someone who must be the whore.

I wait for the sun to completely set so the darkness can hide me as I make my way back to the tunnels to search for Wendy.

CHAPTER 19

We are the Fire

PETER

"Peter... what are you doing?"

I shake my head to clear it and look up into the face of Hook, then down to my bloodied fist.

The whimper from the man I have pressed up against the wall draws my attention and I slowly uncurl my fist from his shirt, holding him in place.

"Where is Wendy?" I bite out as I turn to look at him.

Across the room, I see her speaking with her friend Nicole, and I skirt around the perimeter. When I reach her side, I grasp her arm and drag her with me amidst her protests.

"Peter, let me go, you're hurting me," she whines, and I continue to drag her down one of the tunnels.

Once out of view of the cavern, I press her into the wall, holding her in place with my body.

"Did you, or did you not, leave the tunnels to tell the king where his little whore was?" I hiss.

She doesn't answer me and I move my hand into her hair, gathering a large handful and yanking her head back. I graze her neck with my teeth and bite down just below her ear.

Wendy has learned some new tricks, I realize, when her knee connects with my groin and all the air whooshes out of my lungs. Immediately, I release her and step back, one hand gripping my groin, the other steadying me against the wall.

"You bitch!"

She runs down the tunnel and I remain in my crouched position until I can stand up straight again.

The next day at school, I watch the two of them steal glances at each other throughout the day. One of her annoying brothers comes up to me and starts making small talk. I loathe small talk.

At the end of the day, I watch as again they trail behind while her brothers run ahead.

On my way to my house, I start planning how I'm going to get Wendy, because she will be mine.

Lucia sidles up next to me as soon as I exit the tunnel and I brush her off.

"Hook!" I shout.

His head swivels around the room, and he makes it to me quickly with his long strides. I smirk when I notice the accelerated rise and fall of his chest and flared nostrils. "What did you do to her?" he demands.

"That should be the least of your concerns," I reply.

His fist clenches and unclenches while he gets control of himself. "What are you talking about?"

"Dear Hook, it's about time I show them we are the fire."

"What?"

"But first, I need you to walk the pet."

He rolls his eyes before turning around and making his way down the captive tunnel.

CHAPTER 20

One Too Many

PETER

As soon as he leaves the room, I make my way over to where I know someone has set up something stronger than water. The woman behind the makeshift bar fills a cup for me and slides it across the uneven surface.

The bite of the alcohol is strong as I knock it back and immediately extend my cup for her to refill it again.

Several more times I repeat this before accepting another cup, stumbling over to the wall and sliding down it.

"*Lucia!*" I slur loudly across the room when I see her skirting around the perimeter to me. "I need you to do something for me." An idea forms in my mind.

Wendy's betrayal cuts deep. Even without her confirming that she told the other side of the bitch's location, I know it was her. Wendy has always mostly kept to herself, but there are a few people she would care about something happening to them. And one of those people just so happens to be in my current line of sight.

"What can I help you with, sir?" Lucia asks, kneeling in front of me.

"I need you to get a message to one of my men for me. I seem to be having a little trouble walking." My head lolls to the side as she leaves to pass my message along.

PART SEVEN

He Did What?!

CHAPTER 21

Past the Past

WENDY

J immy doesn't walk with us to school the next day and I can't help but be worried about him. Of the times he's missed school in the past, he usually shows up later with bruises.

Peter meets us outside the school and makes a big show of opening the door for me. My brothers run ahead and take their seats next to each other while I'm still trying to get my scarf, gloves, and coat off.

"Where's Jimmy this morning?" he asks, and I shrug in response. "Huh, he always seems to be with you when you get here."

"Guess he didn't feel like coming to school today." I turn and make my way to the bench I usually share with Jimmy.

Peter follows behind and sits next to me. "If you don't mind, I'll just keep his seat warm."

I face the front, unsure how to respond to his comments.

In the morning, I wake up, and Nicole isn't with me. I decide to go look for her, assuming she's back in the main cavern with everyone. She probably got caught up helping someone or something of the sort.

When I enter the cavern, I don't see her, but I do see Hook and I motion him over to me.

"What's going on?" he asks and I continue to search the room.

"Where's Nicole?" I respond.

"She wasn't with you?"

"If she was with me, I wouldn't be looking for her, now would I?"

He turns, his shoulder touching mine as he searches the room as well. "She was in here a while ago. Last I saw, she was talking to Lucia, then she left."

My head jerks to face him. "Why was she talking to Lucia?"

"I don't know. They were on the other side of the room from me. I assumed when she left, she was going back to where you were."

"James, something is wrong. I can feel it." I wrap my arms around myself, now searching the room frantically for Peter. He probably had something to do with this.

Hook helps me up onto one of the horses from our nearby barn before pulling himself up behind me. He wraps his arms around me to grip the reins.

"Why do you think she's out here?" I ask.

His warm breath skates past my ear as he takes several deep breaths before answering. "I saw several of his men leave just before Lucia was talking to Nicole. If she's not in the caves, my next guess is she left with the men. This is the only horse left, so they must have taken them, too."

He picks up the pace and we fly through the trees. Alternating between galloping and walking to give the horse a break, we eventually run into several riderless horses, some dragging their riders behind them.

Hook dismounts and helps me down.

"What happened here?" My breaths come quicker and I frantically search the fallen people surrounding me.

We glance into every face we pass, Hook bending down to close the eyes that remain open.

"This was a massacre. I think we both know who commanded these men and women to be out here," he bites out.

Making our way through the trees, I recognize Nicole's coat. Tears fall down my face and I freeze in place.

Hook comes up beside me and follows my gaze to where her body lies. He pulls me into his arms while I sob.

"Wendy, I'm so, so sorry," he says over and over again, running his hand up and down my back until they quiet.

"He's going to pay for this. He's going to pay for getting my best friend killed."

"You can't, you can't face him. He's got too many people on his side."

I push against his chest to distance myself from him before turning around and making my way to Nicole. My knees hit the ground and I search for it. "Where is it... Hook? I can't find it!"

"What are you looking for? I can help you look."

"Her necklace. She always wears that necklace. She told me once it was passed down through her family. We have to find it! If we ever get out of this damn place, she'll want her family to have it back."

Hook helps me by lifting the body so I can check the ground beneath her. We search the ground around the clearing, and the necklace is nowhere to be found.

Defeated, I stand and make my way back over to our horse.

"Just take me back."

Hook comes to stand behind me, rubbing my back once more.

"I said, take me back, not comfort me. Let's go."

He nods once before helping me back into the saddle. "Where are we going?"

"To the other side's castle, so I don't get myself killed before I can murder that son of a bitch."

CHAPTER 22

Take Me Away

WENDY

Hook leaves me in the trees not too far from the castle, knowing that his presence would not be appreciated on this side of the invisible line after what he helped Peter do to Callie.

Peter walks with us home after school, and when I notice police cars in front of Jimmy's house, I take off running to make sure he's okay.

The ambulance attendants have him wrapped in a blanket. He stares at the ground and I move toward him. "What happened?"

He looks up at me, and tears streak down either side of his face. I lift my hands to wipe the tears away, waiting for him to give me an answer.

"She's gone."

"Who's gone, Jimmy?"

His eyes are back on the ground, and I kneel, forcing him to look into my eyes.

"My mum." He drops his voice to a whisper before telling me the next part. "He killed her. He finally fucking did it."

. . .

When I make it to the entrance, the castle is abuzz with preparations of their New Year's celebrations. I stand out of the way and wait to see someone I recognize.

Several minutes later, I decide to make my way to the room I usually stay in while I'm here. I'd rather be there and out of the way than for someone to recognize me and ruin the evening for everyone else.

My room still contains all of my things. I quickly change out of my clothes and make my way to the bed, hoping sleep will just take me away. I can talk to them in the morning after they've all had their night of fun.

Instead of sleeping though, memories flash through my head —her beautiful smile, our banter back and forth, how much I'll miss her.

Tears soak the pillow beneath my head until eventually I fall asleep.

CHAPTER 23

World Class F**k Up

HOOK

From the trees, I watch to make sure she gets into the castle under the mountain safely.

I urge my horse into a gallop through the trees until we arrive back at the stables near our tunnels. While brushing the horse down, I attempt to slow my racing heart and mind.

Wendy may be safe, but Peter will most definitely not be as soon as I get my hands on him.

The police come and take Dad away. With all the hospital visits over the years, they tell me he won't be getting out for a very long time. I just can't take the chance. I have to get out of here.

The lights on Wendy's porch are on when I make my way across the street for the last time. Her big brown eyes greet me when she opens the door.

"Hey," she says, her hand still gripped on the handle.

"Hey," I respond, nerves suddenly stealing all the words I had planned on my way over here.

"Would you like to come in?"

"How about we go for a walk?"

"Sure, let me just grab my coat real quick." She closes the door again and appears a moment later with her coat on. "I'll be back soon," she shouts behind her before coming onto the porch and pulling the door closed behind her.

I extend my arm to her, and she places her hand in the crook of my elbow. We stay quiet as we make our way toward the nearby pond and start around the well-worn path.

At the halfway point, I pull her toward the bench the community chipped in to buy and take a seat, pulling her down next to me.

I turn to her and can't seem to remember any of what I wanted to say.

"Jimmy, what's going on? You're scaring me."

"I'm leaving."

"What? Why? I heard your father is going to be in jail for a really long time, possibly forever. Why can't you stay here? Please stay here."

I reach out and start to play with a strand of her long brown hair, which falls around her. "I can't, Wendy. I can't stay in that house." I stop and take a few steadying breaths, clasping my hands together in my lap. "I can't bear to keep living in the house he killed her in," I say to my hands.

"But... where will you go?" She sniffles and I can't bear to look up at her again.

"You!" I shout at him as soon as I enter the cavern. He's holding his own little court here in the damn tunnels.

His smirking face turns toward me, and I close the gap between us in long strides. When I reach him, my hand automatically clenches around his throat and I move in the same direction until I've shoved him down one of the nearby tunnels.

"Where's... Wendy..." he rasps out.

I press my weight into him, further cutting off his air supply. My lips close to his ear, I hiss out, "It seems that you have earned the title of world class fuck up. You better pray to whatever fucked up god you believe in that you never see her again. Your snap decisions got her best friend killed."

His face pales as my words sink in.

"Yeah, so you better just hope that she stays in the castle under the mountain, because if she comes back here, I will watch her gut you."

I give his throat one last squeeze before releasing him and making my way down one of the unused tunnels to listen in on whatever stupid plans he may be making.

CHAPTER 24

Baby's Gone

PETER

Hook's words echo in my head. *Your snap decisions got her best friend killed.* I am now instantly sobered.

It takes me several minutes to pull myself together enough to leave the tunnel. I make my way to my men to continue what we were planning. Not able to focus on anything but Wendy and how the hell I'm going to keep her in my little circle of control, I let the men bounce ideas back and forth, vaguely listening.

At some point, her brothers make their way to our little circle and I'm surprised to see them.

I never thought she would have left her brothers behind. That's why I spent all my goddamn time tormenting her with them. If she left them here with me, she's pissed beyond any point I've ever pushed her to before.

What the fuck am I supposed to do if she doesn't come back? I'll be alone forever, or worst, I'll be stuck with Lucia.

Breaking the Model

WENDY

My eyes are swollen when I finally open them. The castle is quiet and I change into clean clothes and slowly make my way out of the room.

From the silence, I assume Callie has gone back to wherever it is she disappears to sometimes, and I head down to the kitchen for some breakfast and to figure out what I'm going to do now.

As I sit munching on some bread and cheese, I get more and more angry at Peter. I start to plot how I'm going to kill him, get rid of him forever.

He'll never see it coming.

The stable horses are available to anyone who wants to ride, so no one thinks it's strange when I tack one up and head out.

It's still early in the day when I start off. I packed some food for the journey before leaving, so halfway there, I stop at the water's edge and eat my lunch.

. . .

The next day, a knock at the door pulls me from my thoughts and I'm surprised to see Jimmy standing there wearing a naval uniform.

"What? How?" I ask. All other words escape me. He's not old enough, he's my Jimmy, he can't be heading off for the military.

"I told you I'd be leaving. I need to get away. But I wanted to come and say goodbye first."

"No, you can't. Don't leave me here. I... I love you." I admit quietly.

He reaches forward, gently taking my hand and pulling me toward him. "One day... one day I'll come back for you." He runs his fingers back and forth on my face, catching the tears that fall. "And I swear to you when I come back, I will have done what I need to do to deserve you."

"You don't have to go, you can stay, you can live here with us," I plead, even knowing that my parents would never be okay with him moving in here with us.

"We both know that can't happen, Wendy. I promise you, I'll be back. Someday." His hands wind in my hair and he pulls me to him, giving me a too-quick kiss before releasing me and walking to the car that was waiting for him. Several other men stare back at me as I lamely wave goodbye.

I'm able to make it to our castle by nightfall.

Unfortunately, I'm not privy to where they keep the weapons in the castle under the mountain, so as soon as I enter our castle, I make my way to the weaponry.

The easiest things for me to carry are the knives, so I tuck one in the band of my skirt and another up my sleeve before grasping a third in my uninjured hand.

I'm not thinking clearly as I make my way down the hallway and back to my waiting horse.

It's late by the time we reach the tunnels and I lead the horse to the man watching the nearby stables. He takes the horse and leads him inside while I straighten my skirts and make sure all the blades are hidden about my person.

Unlucky for me, I run into Hook before I run into Peter.

"What are you doing back here?" he asks.

I shrug in response, keeping my eyes down.

He reaches out his hand and grasps my chin, gently tipping it up, forcing me to look at him. "I asked what you're doing back here."

"I just can't... he can't get away with this, Jimmy."

He pulls me to him and wraps his arm around me. He leads us down one of the unused tunnels, out of sight of any passersby. "You can't do this. Now is not the time. He hasn't left the cavern with everyone since you left. Do you really want to murder him in front of everyone? In front of the children?"

I let out a sigh of resignation.

"Give them to me," he urges, holding his hands out for my blades.

Reluctantly, I hand him each one.

"How about we stay down here tonight, okay? I'll keep you safe from him."

I nod dumbly and slide down the wall, wrapping my arms around my knees and resting my head on them.

He slides down next to me and wraps his arm around me. His warmth helps to ease some of the tension in my body and I fall asleep tucked against him.

Amen

WENDY

Goosebumps break out on my arms while Hook runs his fingers up and down one. He continues to trail his fingers up to my neck, brushing my brown hair back and repeating his torturous trail up and down, over and over.

"Good morning," he whispers in the silence.

"Morning," I reply. "Now do I get to see him?"

"Have you calmed down?"

I nod, and he cocks an eyebrow. "Okay, maybe not totally calm, but you took all my weapons. Isn't that enough for you to let me talk to him?"

"As long as you know that I won't be leaving you alone with him, sure."

He stands and helps me to my feet before taking my hand and pulling me down the passage after him.

Peter stands in the middle of the cavern talking to some of his men when we enter. His eyes follow us as we make our way to him.

"Wendy would like to talk to you," Hook says.

Peter's eyes never leave me as I stand here silently. "Does she now?" His smirk makes me want to punch him. This time, I know the right way to hold my fist.

Hook leads me across the room, his hand on my waist, while Peter follows close behind.

As soon as we're out of sight of the cavern, I round on Peter, hoping to get the first word in. He stops me in my tracks with, "So, did you come back to apologize?"

My nostrils flare while my mouth falls open in shock. "Excuse me?"

"Did. You. Come. To. Apologize?"

"Oh, I'm so glad to know that I didn't mishear you. What, pray tell, would I need to apologize to you for?" I hold my hand up, silencing him. "Let me make myself clear. I will not now, nor will I ever apologize to you. You killed my best friend. You got mad at me for what? For telling the other side that you had kidnapped one of their people?"

He starts to interrupt me and Hook moves forward and presses him into the wall. "You will stand here and you will listen to everything she has to say. Do you understand me?" His forearm presses into Peter's windpipe and he trails his hook hand down the side of Peter's face.

Wide-eyed, Peter frantically nods his head. Hook lets up some but keeps him pressed against the wall.

"She was my best friend. My *best friend*. And now she's just... gone." I take several deep breaths before continuing. "Ever since we were kids, I have put up with your bullshit. I have let you take advantage of me, blackmail me, and force me to have sex with you. Over and over and over again, you have done whatever the fuck you wanted to. I am done. Do you hear me? I. Am. Done." My body slumps against the wall and I struggle to keep the tears inside.

Hook releases him and pulls me into his arms when Peter speaks.

CHAPTER 27

Broken Girl

PETER

"So we're just going to pretend that I've been a thorn in your side all these years? Like you never enjoyed our time together? Like you didn't come running to me as soon as this one"— I jerk my chin at Hook before continuing—"abandoned you to escape his own demons?"

"You don't know what you're talking about," Hook says.

"Oh, really? Let's see what I know." I tick off on my fingers as I talk. "One, poor little Hook grew up in an abusive home. What? Did Daddy get off on hitting Mummy?"

Hook lunges at me, but Wendy holds him back. Oh, how the tables have turned.

"Two, as you got older, you came to school during the warm months in some of the hottest fucking clothes I've ever seen. What, Daddy wasn't happy just hitting Mummy anymore and came after you? Or did you let him hit you to protect her?"

He falls back into the wall as I continue to smirk, and I continue the onslaught.

"Three, Mummy dearest gets murdered by Daddy and you're

left a pseudo orphan. One parent in the ground, the other parent is in jail for life. Poor little Jimmy, all alone in the world."

I'm surprised when Wendy is suddenly in my face, her finger waving back and forth. Before she can talk, I deliver my final blow.

"Then there's Wendy, the poor little broken girl who just can't be alone. So reliant on others for her own happiness that she sidles up to the next boy in the neighborhood as soon as Jimmy dearest leaves town. How long did it take a week? A month? Before you let me between those soft thighs of yours? Inside that tight, virgin cunt?"

My head jerks to the right when her palm connects with my cheek.

I push her away from me and make my way down the hallway. My work here is now done.

CHAPTER 28

Dead Love Song

WENDY

I sneak past Hook and make my way into the main cavern the next morning. There's one more thing I want to do before I kill this son of a bitch.

The days all go by in a blur. I miss Jimmy more than I ever thought I could. Peter continues to sit next to me and eventually I give in to his persistent begging to go out with him.

I run my hands down my skirt, then twirl it back and forth to make sure it swishes the way I want it to. One more glance in the mirror and I head into the living room to grab my wrap.

"I'll be home before bedtime. Love you guys," I say as I pull my wrap around my shoulders.

"Yeah, yeah, if you and Peter don't run off first," John says.

Mum and Dad both nod to me and smile, and there's a knock at the door. I open it and he extends his arm to me.

"Your carriage awaits, madam," he says with a slight bow of his head.

I can't contain my smile at his chivalry and place my hand on his arm. He leads me to what must be his parents' car where he opens the passenger door for me.

"Where are you taking me tonight?"

"There's this nice spot up the hill. All our friends go there on the weekends."

I don't keep up with the school gossip, always heading straight home with my brothers, so I just nod and he closes the door. It's only a moment later when he is sitting next to me and he struggles to get the car moving.

"Stupid thing never wants to work."

"I've never seen you drive it before. Are you sure you know how?"

"Of course I know how! Just shut up, I've got this."

I don't appreciate his tone. I fold my arms across my chest and purse my lips while he continues to struggle with the car before finally getting it moving.

Hook hid my knives from me, but with almost everyone still sleeping, I'm quickly able to spot several of Peter's men and am able to sneak a couple of blades off their persons. Next to one is a pair of dirty socks and I grab those as well as a length of rope I spot nearby.

Peter is nowhere to be seen in the cavern, so I make my way down one of the tunnels. It takes several tries before I find the right one. I stand in the shadows, watching and waiting for him to wake up.

CHAPTER 29

Like a Rose

WENDY

Lucia stirs first while I'm securing Peter's hands. A gasp escapes her, and I jerk my chin, motioning her to leave. She quickly crawls out of the warmth of their makeshift bed and takes off down the tunnel.

One good thing about her frenzied escape, the noise wakes Peter quickly.

I step forward and lean down, pressing my knee into his chest. Holding the blade to his throat with one hand, I shove the dirty socks into his mouth, holding them there with my injured hand, the pain forgotten in my fury.

His gray eyes widen and I know he's awake enough for me to say what I need to.

I hate Peter. No matter how much I scrub at my skin, I can't remove the dirty feeling left behind.

The other people from school were in various states of undress when we arrived. I stared in shock while one girl from school pressed her bared chest into a boy's hands while his face hid in her neck.

Another boy was moving over a girl while he made grunting noises and she made some kind of squeaking noise.

Some were kissing. That I was familiar with. I didn't want to kiss Peter. I wanted to go home.

I begged Peter to take me back home, insisted that he take me anywhere but here. He refused to leave.

Finally, I stop scrubbing and I pull on my nightgown, make my way outside and throw my torn dress into the garbage can.

In my bed, I lay awake, tears streaming down my face, and I tell myself the story of the island, of Neverland.

"I want to make this clear before I do anything else. You're not making it out of here alive. You understand that, right?"

His eyes grow, and he jerks underneath me. I press the knife further into his throat and he slowly nods.

"You stole something from me all those years ago. And again, every single time you forced me to sleep with you. It wasn't romantic. You didn't save me. You aren't God's gift to mankind. You have always been a weed to society, you suck everything good out of the world and leave behind your poison. But I've finally realized I am the rose. I have been able to thrive despite you constantly taking everything from me. It's time I show you my thorns."

I remove my hand from his mouth and pull out my second blade, slowly bringing my hand around to where I need it. His body bucks beneath me. I turn my head when I hear steps approach me and am surprised to see Hook in the tunnel.

"What do you need me to do?" he asks.

I breathe a sigh of relief. "Hold him down."

Peter goes limp beneath me and Hook takes my place, his knee on Peter's chest, his hook arm pressed into Peter's windpipe and his hand presses the socks deeper.

I move down and undo Peter's pants like he's forced me to so many times before.

He bucks beneath Hook, and I look around him to glance into Peter's terrified face.

A laugh bubbles out of me when it only takes me one determined slice to cut off his most prized body part. Hook looks back as a high-pitched noise comes from Peter.

"Damn," Hook says.

It's like the cork has been removed from my anger and all I can think about is killing him, killing Peter for all he's put me through.

I move up his body and Hook moves out of my way. My hand poised above his chest, my own heaves as I take in deep breaths, doing my best to tamp down the tears threatening to escape me.

"This is for taking my innocence from me." Stab.

"This is for blackmailing me into staying with you." Stab.

"This is for Nicole." A sob escapes me, and the blade doesn't go in as far as my body shakes. Taking a deep breath, I ready myself to finish the job.

"And *this* is for all the years you stole from Hook and me." In one final, long motion, I slice across his throat.

When I look down, I see the blood coating the front of my dress and I wipe my hands as clean as I can on an unsoiled section of my dress.

"We need to get out of here before they find us," Hook says. I glance up to see him standing, hand extended down to me.

PART EIGHT

Life After

CHAPTER 30

Sun Goes Down

WENDY

Hand in hand, we move down the tunnel and emerge in the daylight. Hook looks both ways before we finally exit the tunnel to make sure no one can see our bloodied state.

"We need to get cleaned off before we get horses from the stables. And we need to do it quickly before someone finds his body and alerts the others."

I nod distractedly and he pulls me into the forest.

It doesn't take us long to make it to a stream, and he has me pull my clothes off and get into the freezing water.

"It-t-t-t's cold." My teeth chatter as I quickly wash away the blood from my skin. A weight lifts as I watch the red swirl in the water around me. No more lying to my brothers about my relationship with Peter. I no longer have to be the big sister, protecting them from the most vile human I've come in contact with. I can just...be me.

. . .

I stand on the docks in the cold waiting for Jimmy's ship to enter the port. Peter was off today doing who knows what when I received Jimmy's letter saying he would come home today.

Sailors walk down the ramp onto the dock, and I watch as their families embrace them. The stream of people slows and still, I don't see Jimmy. I grasp the letter to my chest, waiting for him.

When they move around, doing whatever it is they do at the end of a journey, I make my way to a man who looks like he's in charge.

"Excuse me," I say, and his gaze swings to me, clearly irritated by my intrusion. "I'm waiting for a sailor. I didn't see him get off the ship."

His eyes soften and he asks, "What's his name, miss?"

"Jimmy... James Barrie."

He yells over to one of the other men standing closer to the ship, "Hey, Jason, any idea where Barrie went?"

The other man comes over to us and directs his question to me. "Who's asking?"

"Wendy, sir."

"Ah, you're the little woman."

I nod, waiting anxiously for him to tell me what happened to Jimmy.

"He went AWOL, miss. Couldn't find him when we left the last port. We have reported him as missing."

"But I just got a letter from him this morning." I extend the letter to Jason, who takes it from me and looks at the marks on the envelope.

"Yeah, this is postmarked from the last port. He must have run away before we boarded the ship again." He hands the letter back to me before walking back to his post.

"I'm sorry we couldn't be more help," the other man says to me as I turn to leave.

"Thank you for your time," I say quietly and slowly make my way back home.

.   .   .

Hook, who was not nearly as covered in blood as myself, squats near the edge of the river, washing my clothes on a rock.

"Unfortunately, we don't have anything for you to wear until your clothes dry," he says. "But here, this should cover all the important parts." He untucks his shirt from his pants and pulls it off over his head before handing it to me.

I wrap my arms around myself as I start to emerge from the water. Hook's eyes follow my movements as I make my way out. His gaze never leaves mine and my breaths grow ragged as he helps me into his shirt. I sit on a rock and quickly pull my socks and shoes on.

My wet hair falls down my back, and I quickly braid the brown mass and knot the hair around itself at the bottom.

"Come on, let's find somewhere to hang these," he says and he gathers my clothes in his arms.

CHAPTER 31

Love You Now

WENDY

We find a large house nestled in the trees, and judging by the looks of the place when we enter, people have been here recently.

The first thing we do is get a fire going in the fireplace. I rub my hands over my arms, trying to get warm.

Hook hangs my clothes by the fire and I pull off my shoes and socks and rub my feet. The rug in front of the fire is soft and I sit, extending my feet in front of me to absorb some of the warmth from the flames.

He sits in front of me on the rug, pulling my feet into his lap, and begins rubbing warmth into them.

I stare into the flames. "I killed him." It all rushes in and I can't control the sobs wracking my body.

Hook pulls me to him, wrapping me up in his warm embrace. My legs drape across his lap, and he tucks my head under his chin. His hand rubs up and down my back until my breathing grows steady again.

When his hook starts to run up and down my calf, my breath catches. My clit throbs as he moves further and further up my leg.

The smooth metal of his hook eases beneath his shirt I still wear and I glance up to see him watching his hook tease my clit.

I adjust myself in his lap and allow my legs to fall open, giving him easier access. His bare chest is warm against my cheek when I tip my face up to suck on the soft skin of his neck.

I'm unable to stop another memory from surfacing, even while my body sings in Hook's embrace.

I do my best to avoid Peter. He's not a good guy, and the people he surrounds himself with cause trouble.

My parents tell me repeatedly to stop talking to him, and even though I tell them I don't have a choice, they don't believe me.

It's not like I don't see him every single day at school. I've seen the immense pleasure Peter derives from hurting people, picking on them until they break.

I refuse to be the next person in his line of torment. I just have to make it until Jimmy comes back.

"You didn't come back for me," I say.

Hook stills, removing his hook from beneath the shirt I wear and leans back to look into my face. "What?"

"When we were just kids, you said you would be back for me. But you never came. You left me there with him." In my head, I know he is not to blame for what Peter has done to me over the years, but the words fly from my mouth.

"You don't seriously think I left you there willingly, do you?" he questions.

I shake my head frantically and hide my face in his chest.

He wraps both arms tightly around me. "They took me from the docks. I was just about to board the ship home when they took me. The crocodile man and his cronies."

The room grows dark as we sit in front of the dwindling fire, neither of us wanting to get up.

It doesn't take long before the hook is making its way back up my leg again. I moan when it finds my now even more sensitive flesh. He works the rounded metal tip in slow, careful circles. My breaths grow more erratic, and I lean my head back up to continue my assault on his neck when he eases the tip inside me.

His lips capture mine while he continues moving it in and out of me. The curve of his hook presses against places I've never been touched before and I can't help the moan that escapes me.

Our kisses grow more frantic and I run my tongue along the seam of his lips, thankful when he opens to let me in. His tongue reaches out for mine and we both pant as I do anything I can to try to pull him closer to me.

I feel his cock grow harder beneath me and I wiggle against him, reaching across myself to stroke him.

Quickly, the hook is removed from its torturous explorations, and he flips me over onto the rug beneath us. His weight presses me into the soft material.

My hands grasp his back and I dig my nails into the skin, urging him closer.

"I've waited a long time for this and we've got all night," he rasps against my lips.

A shaky breath of anticipation escapes me and he begins his assault on my pussy once more. My body is so worked up it takes less than a minute before it explodes in what I can only describe as fireworks.

As soon as I come down from my high, I reach down and start to undo his pants.

"No, no, you've had a big day. That one was just for you." He kisses me once more before his growling stomach interrupts the silence. "I guess we should see if there is some food somewhere."

I slowly disentangle myself from him and allow him to stand. He extends his hand and helps me up.

The kitchen space has some basic provisions and we work to get a fire going in the stove so we can make something to eat. One cupboard we open contains fresh bread and I tear a chunk off before handing the rest to Hook.

We find ingredients to make a basic stew and we sit at the small table waiting for it to cook.

"Who do you think lives here?" I ask.

He glances around the room before responding, "I don't know. I've passed this place a few times, but rarely see anyone occupying it."

Once our stomachs are full, I make my way back into the front room and pull down my now-dry dress.

Hook follows me. He stops in the doorway and leans against it, arms crossed, and his eyes follow me as I lay my dress on a nearby chair. Slowly, I reach for the hem of the shirt I wear.

In a few strides, he stands in front of me, his hand covering mine to help me with my task.

"Shall we see what this place has in the way of sleeping quarters?" I ask, looking up into his dark eyes.

He releases my hand and raises his to my cheek. His thumb rubs back and forth. When he opens his mouth to speak, I quickly lean up to press my lips to his, silencing whatever he was going to say.

I'm just about to pull back, break contact, when Hook's tongue sweeps in. All thoughts leave me and I pull him closer to me.

He wraps his other arm around me, drawing me into him.

Our breaths come out harder, faster, and I feel that same glorious sensation building.

His hand travels down my body, to my ass, and he pulls me against him. A moan escapes me, shocking me enough I immediately pull back, my hands now pressing him away.

"What... what was that?" I pant.

He smirks and shrugs before replying, "I just can't help myself. You've grown into an incredible woman. You know that, right?"

I grasp his hand and pull him after me down the hallway. The tingling in my belly grows the further down the hall we get. The first door we come to, I glance inside and heave a sigh of relief when I see a bed.

The emotions of the day bubble over and I can't tamp down the surge of lust I feel toward this man I've been in love with most of my life.

As soon as the door closes behind me, Hook pushes me up against it, lifting me by my butt and I wrap my legs around his waist. I have done this before, many times with Peter. But never has it felt this way, never have I felt this absolute sense of urgency to have a cock buried deep inside.

This somehow feels different from what we did just a short time ago.

I gasp when his length presses against me, right where I want him.

He continues kissing me as I'm pressed against the door, and I tug him closer to me. It only takes him a few strides to get me to the bed, and he lays me down on the soft surface.

I watch as he removes his shoes, unlaces his pants, and tugs them down his legs.

Frantically, I tug Hook's shirt off over my head.

When we're both naked, we spend a few moments just taking each other in. I lean up onto my elbow and use my other hand to softly touch his erect cock. He's so much bigger than Peter, and I wonder briefly if he'll fit.

He hisses in a breath and covers my hand with his own. "I'm going to come like a damn teenager if you keep doing that."

I pull my hand back and scoot my way up the bed to the pillows. He joins me, his body warming my side. His hand runs small circles over my abdomen.

"I never thought we would get here," I say, reaching my hand up and running my fingers through his soft brown hair.

He grasps my hand and kisses the palm before moving over me. "I want you to know, all those years ago, I didn't say it, but I loved you, too. Hell, I still love you now."

I pull him down to me and kiss him deeply. My hands run over the muscles of his back and my core throbs, needing something... more.

He holds himself at my entrance and pulls back, staring into my eyes. Watching me. Waiting.

"I never stopped loving you." A tear runs down my cheek and he wipes it away before kissing me once again.

His head teases my entrance and I reach down, and with both hands on his firm ass, I pull him toward me.

Slowly, he inches forward. Just the tip enters me and he waits for me to adjust to his size before he pushes forward an inch more and then pulls almost all the way out, and then repeating the action.

His tongue slides into my mouth, plunging into it in rhythm with his cock. Over and over and over again, he continues his slow pace.

When I think my body can't take any more, a loud moan escapes me when he is finally all the way inside.

His lips stop their glorious assault, and he lifts his upper body to look down at me. "I want to look into your eyes as I make love to you for the first time."

I bite my lower lip and nod once. He pulls almost all the way out again before slowly moving in again. We both groan at the feel of each other after all these years of waiting.

"I knew we'd be a perfect fit," he says, continuing the slow movements.

The way he moves his body hits my clit perfectly, in a way I've never felt before. The feeling in my lower belly continues to grow.

A few more slow strokes in and out, and I think I might combust. He sucks one of my nipples in deep, and I swear I see stars as I explode, wrapping my arms around him and pulling him to me.

He moves faster, his motions more erratic, and finally a low groan escapes him. "That was..."

"Amazing?" I suggest.

He kisses the tip of my nose before pulling out to lie beside me, facing me while I still lie on my back. His fingers play with my hair when he says, "I'm so deeply sorry."

"For what?"

"Leaving you with him. Not coming back to you. Not fighting for you once we got here."

I move onto my side to face him. "None of that was your fault. Peter was... a terrible kid who turned into an even worse man. We all had our own paths we had to take to get here."

CHAPTER 32

End of the World

HOOK

Once we're both dressed, it's time we find somewhere better to settle. Wendy insists we head to the castle under the mountain. I can't help but wonder if they'll kill me on sight for what I was forced to do to Callie.

I lift Wendy onto the horse before pulling myself behind her. My cock hardens, knowing there is just a small space separating it from its new favorite place.

"Something I can help you with?" she coyly asks, looking at me over her shoulder.

I pinch her side, making her giggle before clucking to the horse and starting our short trek to the mountain.

About halfway there, I just can't help myself. Not knowing if they're going to imprison me immediately, I stop the horse and dismount.

"What are you doing?" Wendy asks.

"You'll see," I reply, leading the horse carrying her to a nearby tree and helping her down.

"What—"

She stops talking when I press her against the tree, my hand quickly releasing my cock from my pants.

Her eyes grow wide when I use both my hand and my hook to pull her skirts up.

"Wrap your arms around my neck and don't let go," I say. Quickly, she complies and I lift her, urging her legs to wrap around me. In one plunge, I'm seated inside her and we both let out a sigh.

Immediately upon arriving, one man grasps our horse's reins, and another man comes out of a hidden door.

"Theodore, this is my friend, James..." Wendy starts.

He watches me before I feel my arms grasped from behind.

"Wait, no! What are you doing?" she asks.

I hang my head, knowing that somehow, this man I've never met before knows that I was involved in what happened to their king's woman.

"It's okay, Wendy. I'll just go with him and explain everything. I'll be with you soon. I'm sure of it." I say, hoping I'm not lying to her again.

I stole from the crocodile man. That's when he cut off my hand.

They told me some shit about looking like a proper pirate now, even let me pick my own damn name. I remember that name from Wendy's story so long ago. "Captain Hook," I reply.

"Captain? You're no captain," he spits, the long reddish-brown beard soaking up some of the liquid. "But sure, we can call you Hook the Powder Monkey. Does that suit you?"

I nod my head numbly, knowing I'll have to play their game if I have any hope of making it back to Wendy.

. . .

They lead me to the cells and leave me there. Thankfully, it isn't long before the man, Theodore, shows back up.

"You know why you're here, of course?"

I nod my head.

"You said you would explain. I'm listening." He sits cross-legged on the floor.

"Everything I have done, I have done for that woman. I will do whatever I have to do to keep her safe until my dying breath."

He watches me before asking, "What was your reason for attacking Callie?"

"I was ordered to."

"I don't know what goes on over there on your side of things, but you seem to be ordered, and comply, I might add, with doing some of the most reprehensible things. First, Wendy is ordered to kill our king, now you are ordered to beat up one of our people."

He remains silent for a moment before standing and leaving. When he returns, there is another man with him and I watch Theodore lean in close and whisper something in his ear.

The man makes his way to the bars where I stand, grasping one bar in my hand, waiting for their verdict. I may not be able to protect Wendy anymore after this, but at least now she doesn't have to deal with that asshole, Peter.

He leans in close and inhales deeply through his nose before turning around and speaking with Theodore in hushed tones and leaving down the tunnel, alone.

"According to Zev, you do not smell like deceit. We will release you on one condition: You two will not remain in the castle. You can stay at the house you occupied last night."

"How—" I break off when he raises his hand to silence me.

"I also talked to Wendy. She did not know you were involved in Callie's abuse. But she says she knows you would never have hurt her of your own volition. So while I will not allow you to stay in the castle, you can remain in the cabin. If you two need anything, Wendy may request provisions from James or Steve, who will live in the house periodically on their scouting missions.

"I also expect you to add on an additional room to replace the one you two will occupy. We will provide you with the tools and send a man to help you."

My mouth hangs open and I nod dumbly.

He leans in close before finishing, "If I find out that you are abusing any more of our people, you will be killed. Do we understand each other?"

"Yes, sir." I reply, and he brings the keys out of his pocket, releasing me from the cell.

It takes me several years, but I'm able to work my way up the ranks. Eventually taking over when the crocodile man leaves the boat for true love or some shit.

One of our trips took us close to home, and I left my crew aboard the ship before making my way to the last place I saw her.

When we emerge from the tunnel, she turns around, and a smile stretches across her face. She runs, throwing herself at me. I wrap my arms around her, laughing at her exuberance.

"Not to rush you or anything, but you two need to be gone before the king realizes you're here."

I nod to Theodore one last time before following him down the long tunnel to freedom.

CHAPTER 33

Life Like This

WENDY

Months fly by and Hook and the man they sent to help make good time on the new bedroom.

I spend my days working the little garden we've been able to cultivate near our home.

When Hook is not working on the new addition, he's building things like chicken coops and small stables so we can be self-sufficient out here.

I toss the chickens their breakfast, scattering the grain and smiling as they crowd the area. Once all the chickens have vacated the nest, I take the opportunity to pull any fresh eggs out, placing them into the pockets of my apron.

We've hosted James and Steve a few times when they've been exhausted from a mission, but they just left this morning, so we don't expect them back for some time.

I make my way back inside and can't help but watch him. Hook sits on one of the chairs at the table, working on repairing one of our traps.

He looks up when I approach and smiles at me. "Can I help you, Wendy, dearest?"

My hands tremble slightly in anticipation as I place the eggs in one of our bowls and make my way over to him. "There might be a little something..." I trail my hand across his shoulders, and he sets the net on the table, leaning his head back to watch me behind him.

"Oh, really? And what would that be?" Hook pushes himself back from the table and starts to rise.

I push him back into the chair and lift my skirts up.

Hook slowly unlaces his pants and pulls them down. His cocks bobs free and I smile, knowing how much pleasure we're in for.

He helps me settle over him and holds his cock at my entrance. I drop down onto him, the sudden invasion taking my breath away.

"Goddamn, woman, you're going to ruin me. You know that, right?"

I bite my lip and slowly lift and lower myself on his shaft. "I can stop now, if you'd prefer?"

"Fuck, no," he says emphatically. "If you even attempt to stop, I'll be forced to punish you."

"Oh, really? And just what punishment were you thinking?" I blink my lashes and hold back a laugh. Hook doesn't scare me one bit.

"I might just make you marry me."

"Yes, please," I reply.

His hand tangles in my hair and he pulls my mouth to his, our kisses messy and unapologetic, just like our journey to get here.

A couple of hours later, Steve and James come rushing into the house and I wipe the flour off my hands from the bread I was working on.

"What's going on?" I ask.

"There are people arriving," James pants.

"Our scouts finally came back," Steve continues.

Hook comes into the other room from where he was putting the finishing touches on the new bedroom. "How can we help?"

Acknowledgments

First and foremost, thank you to my family for always being supporting of whatever I want to do.

Thank you to my alpha readers, who patiently waited for me to finish the first draft so they could give me valuable feedback.

Thank you to my beta readers for kindly (or not) helping me make my book better. You guys will always be the real MVP's!

Thank you to my editor, who amazingly got the book back to me in about twelve hours!

Thank you to all of the authors in the BookTok Community, and those willing to come on my podcast, Freya's Fairy Tales. Your tips, tricks, and other advice helped me get to where I am.

And Finally, thank you to each and every one of you for picking up a book written by me. I will be forever grateful that you took a chance on me!

Also, yes, I did reuse most of this from the first book because my team is still the best!

About the Author

Freya Victoria is a Texas native that has always wanted to write her own books and has spent countless hours attempting to write, reading books from every genre, and has been reading aloud, with all the character voices, since she was a kid. Growing up, Freya always struggled to come up with a storyline that she could develop into a full novel but, she finally found an idea that stuck. You can find Freya every day in the recording booth, working on someone's audiobook, working on more podcast episodes, or sitting on the couch reading and writing. She resides in Texas with her husband and daughter and hopes to one day move into the country where she can not have to edit out the sound of her neighbors mowing their lawn or the trash truck as it drives by!

ABUSIVE RELATIONSHIPS

Hook grows up in an abusive household (father is a drunk and abuses both his mother and him, eventually killing her)

Peter is an asshole and some of his actions are considered abusive or manipulative

ALCOHOL

Multiple characters drink, both recreationally and destructively

ASSAULT

Hook's mother is beaten and killed. Hook is also abused as a child. Peter is rough many times with his sexual partners.

BULLYING

Peter is a narcissistic sadist. He will do whatever he needs to to get what he wants.

CHEATING

Wendy does not want to be Peter's "girlfriend" he does have her in a semi-committed fuck-buddy situation. While she is away from the castle, he has sex with another woman.

CHILD ABUSE

Hook's father is abusive. He is later imprisoned for killing Hook's mother.

DEATH & MURDER

This book tells the villain's side from The Forgotten Beast. There is war related death, along with the murder of Hook's mother (not on page).

EMOTIONAL ABUSE

Peter is constantly blackmailing Wendy into being with him. He continually threatens her with her brothers' lives.

RAPE

This includes both non-con (not on page), and dub-con (every time he tells Wendy do this... or else)

SEXUALLY EXPLICIT SCENES & LANGUAGE

The Forgotten Island is a fantasy romance book. It is a childhood friends to lovers story and there are less romantic scenes spread throughout with romantic explicit scenes toward the end. Profanity is nothing more than you'd hear out in public.